Praise for Robert Campbell and

THE GIFT HORSE'S MOUTH

A Jimmy Flannery Mystery

"Robert Campbell is an awfully good writer."
—Elmore Leonard

"Jimmy Flannery, sewer inspector extraordinaire, is back in his element. . . . solving the crime is what he is good at and . . . he does it with the style that only a Chicago shuffler could accomplish. . . . A lot of action, a dandy mystery."
—*Ocala Star-Banner*

"Campbell does a fine job of capturing the flavor of working-class Chicago, and Jimmy and company are some of the most appealing characters ever to appear in print. As usual, Campbell doesn't stint on the humor. . . ."
—*Rave Reviews*

"Reading a Flannery caper is always fun. . . ."
—*Chicago Tribune*

Books by Robert Campbell

Alice In La-La Land
The Gift Horse's Mouth
Juice
Nibbled To Death By Ducks
Plugged Nickel
Red Cent

Published by POCKET BOOKS

Most Pocket Books are available at special quantity discounts for bulk purchases for sales promotions, premiums or fund raising. Special books or book excerpts can also be created to fit specific needs.

For details write the office of the Vice President of Special Markets, Pocket Books, 1230 Avenue of the Americas, New York, New York 10020.

ROBERT CAMPBELL

THE GIFT HORSE'S MOUTH

POCKET BOOKS

New York   London   Toronto   Sydney   Tokyo   Singapore

This book is a work of fiction. Names, characters, places and incidents are either the product of the author's imagination or are used fictitiously. Any resemblance to actual events or locales or persons, living or dead, is entirely coincidental.

POCKET BOOKS, a division of Simon & Schuster Inc.
1230 Avenue of the Americas, New York, NY 10020

Copyright © 1990 by Robert Campbell

ISBN: 0-671-74340-6

First Pocket Books paperback printing September 1991

10 9 8 7 6 5 4 3 2 1

POCKET and colophon are registered trademarks of
Simon & Schuster Inc.

Printed in the U.S.A.

THE GIFT HORSE'S MOUTH

• 1 •

I GOT FRIENDS who tell me, "Jimmy, wake up, the world's passing you by" or "Flannery, the old dog is dead, can't you smell it? Get your shovel out and bury the poor thing."

The world which they tell me is passing me by is the opportunity for a promotion to supervisor—maybe even to the top job—in the Sewer Division of the Department of Streets and Sanitation in the great city of Chicago.

The old dog what is dead is the Democratic Party machine, which, some say, took the setup jab in 1968 when Daley and the national Party leaders indulged in a cursing match on television, the knockout punch when he told the Chicago police to fire on looters and arsonists after the assassination of Martin Luther King, and got the count after Mayor Bilandic, Daley's successor, lost the fifth floor to Jane Byrne because he couldn't get the winter snows of '79 off the streets.

Even though Jane hugged the old guard after the race she'd run and won against the machine, they never really forgave her for it. They gave her lukewarm support when she ran for reelection in '83; she lost to Harold Washington and the reform ticket.

That's the first time everybody told me the old machine was rusted and busted.

If you think a political machine's an organization what can deliver the votes for a candidate no matter how bad he or she may be, then I suppose there ain't a machine left in any major city in the country. If you think, like I think, that a machine's a way for the people to get a little room at the public trough, then the machine's alive and it'll always be alive because there's always going to be somebody who can't help themselves; who ain't got a clue how to go about it; who're going to go to somebody like me for help.

I know how to pull the strings and push the buttons, cut the deals and trade favor for favor.

That's how it is, that's how it's always been and that's how it'll always be; I don't care what you call it.

I work inspecting the sewers not because I particularly like it but because I got to make a living. Even though my old Chinaman, Delvin, put me in the spot because I was ready, willing, and able to work for the Democratic Party in the Twenty-seventh Ward, I ain't one of them political appointees who just stops by the office to collect his pay.

And I ain't one of them people like Kippy Kerner, who spent twenty years supervising another guy who checked the steam valves at City Hall. He was ready to take retirement when he dropped dead of a stroke right on the job. Some of the wags down at the Hall say it was because the valve-checker called in sick and Kippy Kerner had to do the job hisself. When he bent over to read a dial, the blood rushed to his head and that was that.

Also we got Billy Swinarski, who sits in front of the

city treasurer's office telling people where is the city treasurer's office. Hizzoner, the late Richard J. Daley, put Billy there for good reason. Billy had got hisself injured on Daley's behalf in an election dispute, and him sitting there, gainfully employed, let everybody who ever walked into the Hall know that with Hizzoner loyalty was a two-way street.

Nobody's ever got around to showing Billy the door after Daley died. By now it'd be like knocking down the Water Tower. Billy's a public treasure.

So, anyway, whether the machine is dead or not—no matter who wins the election what's coming up with Mayor Washington dead and gone, God rest his soul—the party, old or new, has got to have people knocking on doors and precinct captains telling them how to do it. Also somebody like me what can get a tree trimmed if it's blocking the sun coming in an old person's kitchen window in the morning or get the water turned on if a mother of four can't even flush because her man walked out on her and she can't pay the bills or work the welfare system fast enough.

My old man, Mike Flannery, who was a precinct captain for years while he was in the fire department, tells me that if I want to hang on to the idea that the machine is still operating or might even be coming back, then it's about time that I say yes to old Delvin, who wants to retire and turn the ward over to me.

Which means he'd be handing over an empty sock at this minute because I turned down the chance to run for alderman once, and to be committeeman without being alderman don't count for a hell of a lot anymore. When I took a pass a while back, they ran somebody else and a lipstick lesbian by the name of Janet Canarias put together a coalition what won the seat against the party candidate.

She's still in it, doing a great job. Also she's a very good friend.

But I think that maybe it's about time I say okay and take the title for the honor of it or to please my friends and family—my father, my wife, my mother-in-law, my aunt by marriage, my dog, and the kid who lives across the hall—if for no other reason.

Also it's time for me to get a step up in the job and an increase in pay. Mary tells me a couple of months ago that we're going to have a baby and that's the best reason I know for a man to get some ambition.

Which lands me on Delvin's doorstep on a bright, windy day in November.

For a minute there, when his housekeeper, Mrs. Thimble, opens the door, I get a sharp little pain. For years it was Mrs. Banjo—God keep her—was his housekeeper who opened the door and always had something to scold me about.

When she passed away she left me a city lot to build a house on for Mary and me, but we had to sell it to save the old block of flats we live in. But that's another story.

The point is I'm standing there with the leaves blowing right up the steps to the porch and past me into the vestibule when Mrs. Thimble says, "Well, come in if you're coming in, Mr. Flannery. You're letting half the dirt in the city blow into my clean house."

Which makes me feel better.

"The master's in the parlor counting his toes," she says with this bitter way she's got of talking.

"Can I go right on in?"

"Well, if you expect me to announce you, you've got another think coming," she says. "I did that for old Father Mulrooney and look what it got me."

I don't want to point out that her announcing visitors in the priest's house didn't cause his death or lose her

her job, but I decide to let it go and just slip on past her into the overheated hallway, where Delvin's ancestors stare out at me from photographs the color of strong tea, and then on into the parlor.

Delvin's dozing in his chair. He's got a belly as big as a wheelbarrow but he's lost a lot of weight around the neck and chest the way some old people do. There's hardly any color in his face. It hits me that he ain't got long to live. I thought that before and he fooled me and everybody else, including his doctors, but this time I think I got it right.

I sit down in the chair opposite him in the gloomy room. Every shade's been pulled down almost to the sills and half the drapes are closed.

I sit there for a long time just looking at him, rolling back the years in my head. That's making me blue so I clear my throat enough times that he finally starts and opens his eyes, looking right at me.

"Did Mrs. Thimble offer you a little refreshment?"

"I don't want anything," I says.

"That may be, but she should've asked. That woman's going to ruin the reputation of my house."

If he means the reputation that Delvin's hospitality is thinner than the seat of beggars' drawers, there's not much danger. The only reason he sees to it that I get served a little something is because I don't drink hard liquor and he gets to have his and mine as well. But seeing the way he looks, I decide I'll drink the damned toddy this time just to keep him from swigging it.

"Cold out, is it?" he goes on.

"Not too bad."

"Blowing a wind though?"

"Well, it is that."

"So you must feel a bit nippy. Mrs. Thimble!" He gives out a yell fit to wake the dead. Then does it twice more.

She takes her good old time coming and then just stands there waiting for him to say what's on his mind.

"My friend, Jim here, needs something to warm him up."

"Cocoa?" she says.

"Nothing you got to cook. You'd only burn it. Bring us two whiskeys and branch water without the ice."

She blinks her watery eyes three or four times like she's working up a protest but never delivers it. She just walks out with a sharp nod of her head.

"So while we're waiting, what have you got to tell me?" Delvin says.

"I've come to tell you I accept," I says.

A little smile turns up the corners of his mouth a bit. It's a look a cat would get when it saw a bottle of cream on the stoop, except they don't hardly deliver milk anymore.

"Accept what?" he says when waiting me out don't look like it's going to work.

"You've made me offers in the past."

"I recall."

"Are they still good?"

"What do you think? The alderman's job is in that woman's pocket. The leader's job in the ward don't mean a hell of a lot without you're also the alderman, but even so, it might not be mine to offer at the moment."

"How's that?"

"There's an election coming up, haven't you heard? People are choosing up sides. Ray Carrigan, as head of the Party, is gathering his cards for the showdown hand."

"What's the Twenty-seventh to him?"

"It's sitting cheek to cheek with the First and The Loop."

"The last movie house closed in the Loop just a couple of weeks ago. That could be the beginning of the end for the First."

"Use your head. The Loop's going banking and commercial and that's got more clout than movie houses, nightclubs, and sin any day of the week. So if banking and financial spreads, where's it going to spread? Into the Twenty-seventh along Washington and Randolph is where."

"You telling me I got to go to Carrigan and bend the knee?"

"You bend the knee when Mary gets you to go to church, and you ain't believed in that for years. You bend the knee when you go to see the cardinal and kiss his ring."

"That's tradition. That's ceremony," I says.

"That's all I'm saying," he snaps back.

Delvin stirs himself as Mrs. Thimble comes back into the room with a tumbler in each hand.

"My God, woman, don't you know enough to serve guests on a tray? Especially when you're offering a drink to your benefactor, the man who got you the position you enjoy in this house?"

She snorts through her nose like a cat and hands a glass to each of us, letting Delvin know she ain't going to wipe a tray for two drinks, and letting me know she don't appreciate the job I got for her all that much.

"Where was we?" Delvin asks after he takes a pretty good belt out of his glass.

"I was on my knees in Carrigan's office."

"I know there's no love lost. I know there's old business between you, favors refused, monkey wrenches tossed in the machinery. But he ain't put you in the freezer yet. You understand what I'm saying?"

I take a sip of my drink and Delvin's eyebrows twitch.

"You saying he wants me on his books?"

"That's right. He's helped you now and then because I asked him to do the favor for me. But he wants you to ask a favor."

· 7 ·

"So you're saying his door's open waiting for me to walk in?"

"That's what I'm saying could be the case."

"All right, then, if I got to do it, I'll do it."

"The sooner, the better," Delvin says. "Why don't you trot right on over to his office now?"

He's finished his toddy and has his eye on mine. I take another short swallow.

"Which office?" I asks.

"Tuesdays, Ray's at his main office on State. As long as you catch him before noon."

"Shouldn't I make a call first?"

"Take my word, it's all right. He asks you, tell him you come unannounced because I told you it'd be okay to come unannounced."

That way Delvin will know how he stands in Carrigan's esteem without having to ask. He sees me without an appointment, on Delvin's say-so, it means Delvin's still wearing power suspenders. He don't and it could mean they've already wrote Delvin off and are just letting him hang around until he keels over.

It could also mean that Carrigan's busy or wants me to do it by the numbers, but Delvin already knows that. Half of politics is testing the water when it don't cost you nothing.

I stand up, ready to go.

"If you say so, I'll go right on over," I says.

"Then you won't be needing your toddy, will you?" Delvin says, and snatches the glass right out of my hand.

• 2 •

NOBODY KNOWS how many offices Ray Carrigan keeps around the city, county, and state. He's been into real estate, commodity options, magazine distribution, publishing, printing, politics, and other assorted enterprises for forty years, and it seems like he wants to keep every interest separate from every other one. Like he don't want his left hand to know what his right hand is doing.

Johnny McAfee, who knows Carrigan better than maybe anybody else—they've been friends or friendly enemies since they was kids in kindergarten—says it's Carrigan's way of writing off the expenses of his girlfriends.

I been in maybe three of Carrigan's offices at one time or another. None of them are anything lavish. He's not trying to impress. But in every one of them he's got a good-looking receptionist sitting behind the desk. Mostly all they're doing is their nails, but they all got great legs so that's all right, too.

Only one of them ever seemed to do much of anything. Goldie Hanrahan.

For thirty of those forty years you had to get past Goldie if you wanted to see Carrigan.

The first five years he was easy to get to. He was just starting out building his empire and you could just knock on the door and walk in. Then he got Goldie out front and she made it very difficult for anybody and everybody, even the mayors, except for Hizzoner, Dick Daley.

The last five years Goldie's been retired and he's got nobody at the front desk in the main office sorting people out. Just some doll with great legs doing her nails and maybe picking up the phone to tell him who's waiting.

In the old days, if you got in to see Carrigan, he looked at you surprised, like he forgot he told Goldie to let you in, like she hadn't stopped you outside and listened to your spiel, then told you no soap.

Nowadays, you can tell he misses her a lot.

They say she was so pretty in her younger years she could stop your heart. In spite of having bad teeth which showed a lot of fillings. They didn't call her Goldie because she had yellow hair and a pretty face. It was because the fillings and crowns was gold. You could see the little edges of the crowns and bridges when she smiled. Which she did a lot even when she was sweeping you out the door.

Also she favored gold in other things.

People tried to bribe Goldie to put them up on the appointment list or get on the list at all, but she never took any bribes.

Gifts she'd take.

There were four holidays she favored. Christmas, St. Patrick's Day, her birthday in June, and the feast of St. Wenceslas on September 28, which, since he's the patron saint of Czechoslovakia and Goldie's Irish, don't signify nothing except his day fills the gap between June and December very nicely.

The gifts of choice was gold, Florentined, inlaid, hammered, chased, or cast—nothing filled or washed. If you didn't come with gold, she'd accept cash in a discreet greeting card or maybe some stock in a blue-chip company. Nothing gaudy, just substantial.

I always get a funny feeling that things ain't quite right when I walk into Carrigan's State Street office and Goldie ain't sitting there. It's like it's another sign that the world's falling apart.

Anyway, after I tie my dog, Alfie, up to a fire hydrant —he shouldn't get taken short in the car and be uncomfortable in case I got to stay awhile—I take the elevator up to the fifteenth floor and go into Carrigan's outer office.

The young woman doing her nails behind the reception desk is a redhead I never seen before.

There's an aristocratic-looking, medium-sized poodle with a fancy haircut laying down on its own little rug. It half raises its head and gives me the old one-eye, but I ain't important enough to bother with so it settles right down again with a little snort.

"My name's Jimmy Flannery and I'd like to see Mr. Carrigan," I says.

"You got an appointment?"

"No, but if you tell him Jimmy Flannery's here, I'm pretty sure he'll see me."

"Mr. Carrigan's a busy man," she says, and gives me this little wink. Which I don't know what it means—is she saying he's not a busy man, he's a busy man where she's concerned, or he's not a busy man where she's concerned and would I like to give her a little action? It's either that or she's got a fleck of mascara in her eye.

"Maybe if you hit the button and ask him how busy he is at the minute we could both find out," I says.

"Oh, sure, that's easy for you to say," she says, giving me this little smile.

"I think I missed the train," I says.

"Nap time. It's Mr. Carrigan's nap time."

"Since when does the Chairman take a nap in the middle of the morning?"

"Since he turned eighty-two last week," she says.

"My God," I says, "I forgot all about his birthday."

All of a sudden the redhead looks sad, like she's been thinking that one over for a long time. "You ain't the only one."

I'm about to say that maybe I should come back another time when the intercom on her desk squawks. For maybe half a minute there's a lot of throat clearing and coughing like static and then Carrigan's whiskey tenor says, "What time is it, Marilyn?" Before she can answer he goes on, "Let's turn up the heat a little, it's like an icebox in here. How about a cup of coffee and put a little antifreeze in it. Hurry it up, get in here and let me give you a little pat on the ass."

She writes everything he asks for down on her pad in handwriting you'd need a magnifying glass to read. She numbers each item including the last as though she wants to prove her efficiency.

"His last request is more like a reflex," she says, giving me that little smile again. "It's been months since he could do anything substantial."

"You had a shot there to tell him I'm waiting out here."

"Let me go in and turn up his thermostat," she says, giving it the double meaning, "and I'll tell him in person."

As she gets up and goes into Carrigan's office, the view from where I'm sitting is very nice.

This good-looking young woman is going in to do for a man who probably don't even appreciate her anymore even if he does like to pat her on the bottom for old times' sake.

I wondered what you could offer an old player like Ray Carrigan who's had the power for forty years or more, all the money he can ever spend, and women he can't even sing the song with anymore.

After a couple of minutes, she sticks her head out the door, peeking around it with one leg cocked back like she's a stripper teasing the crowd from behind the curtain. "Mr. Carrigan'll see you now and wants to know if you'd like a cup of coffee, too."

I walk over to the door. She straightens up and holds it open for me.

"Marilyn," Carrigan says, "after you bring the coffee go take Mistinguette for a walk."

She nods and goes to make the coffee as I walk over to shake Carrigan's hand.

He looks like a gnome with thistledown for hair, standing behind the big oak desk with the morning sun slanting through the blinds. His cheeks are red and his eyes are blue and he don't look like an eighty-year-old man who just woke up from a nap.

"Sit yourself down, Jimmy," he says, sitting down hisself and looking at the palm of his hand like it held a bag of wonders. "You just shook the hand that patted the ass of Marilyn O'Connell."

"Well," I says.

"Shocked are you, Flannery? I always thought you had a touch of blue around your nose. Always wanting to do what's right, what's proper, what's becoming. A great lover of tradition you Flannerys are. Your father never played around with the ladies and wouldn't take a free ride, even though he was a fireman."

He's giving me the jab because I refused his favors more than once and outsmarted him more than twice. If one thing old politicians don't forget is a favor, the other thing they remember even longer is an insult. They'll pay back the favor once. They'll get back the insult a thousand times in little ways.

"Marilyn's grandmother was my sweetheart back in fifth grade. Her mother was my mistress after her no-good old man took off on her and five kids twenty-five years ago. Now Marilyn's my receptionist. You want to talk tradition, that's tradition, Flannery."

"I'm sure the O'Connells remember you in their prayers," I says in a respectful voice.

"And the Danahers. And the Ryans. That was her grandmother's name, Kate Ryan." He falls into a dreamy state. "I've got my memories, Jimmy," he says in a softer voice.

Marilyn comes back into the room with the coffee and walks out again, Carrigan's eyes on her all the way, like a man watching a boat with his dearest treasure aboard taking off from the dock out into the endless sea.

"Nothing in yours, Jimmy," he says, taking a swallow of his coffee. "I remembered you don't indulge."

"I wish I had a memory like yours, Mr. Carrigan."

"Yes, memories," he says, still thinking of Kate Ryan and her daughter who was a Danaher.

He takes a swallow of coffee, puts it down, picks up the watch fob on his vest with one hand, and taps his forehead with the finger of his other hand.

"Good head for numbers, too, Jimmy. I reckon, in spite of red marks here and there, you're still good on my books. So what can I do for you?"

"I'm glad to hear you say that, Mr. Carrigan, because I'm here to get your blessing."

"For what, Jimmy? For what?"

"Mr. Delvin wants to put some of his burdens down. He thinks I could do the job."

"What job's that?"

"Committeeman of the Twenty-seventh."

"That's a very important job," he says, like we're talking about a working gold mine when all the time we both know the job is no more than ceremonial since the reformers took the power away from the true Democratic Party.

There's even a look in his eye that's asking how come I even want the title since I got pretty good relations with the incumbents at the Hall and maybe it's because I know something he don't know, which, even at his age, is hardly possible. Then he smiles like he's found the pot of gold under the roots of the old oak tree. He thinks he's figured it out. I want to be warlord of the Twenty-seventh for insurance. Hizzoner's boy could win the mayor's race and old connections could become platinum again.

"Are you sure you want the responsibility?" he says, reminding me once again that I turned down the offer to run for alderman once and let a woman with unnatural desires for other women snatch the prize.

"I don't know if it's even a question of wanting it, Mr. Carrigan," I says. "I figure I got to take it if Mr. Delvin offers it, because if I don't, somebody else will and he'll have his own friends, his own people to work with, and maybe it turns out I'm not even a precinct captain anymore but just a worker knocking on doors and stuffing envelopes. Which I don't for one minute mind doing for the Party except I've been taking care of my people in the neighborhoods for a long time now and . . ."

He clasps his hands together on the desk and leans over them. "Jimmy, Jimmy," he says, as though he's talking to a retarded child, "haven't you looked around lately? The Loop lost its last movie house. The nightclubs are going to rot. The Irish and the Italians and the Jews have moved out of the neighborhoods to Evanston and Skokie. Your neighborhoods are going black."

"The blacks are my people, too, Mr. Carrigan," I says, not even liking to say it because it sounds like I'm pinning a rose on myself.

He leans back in his chair. "Let me think about it," he says, making out like the favor I'm asking is a big one and not really a very small favor, indeed. That's the way a politician works sometimes, selling you plated tin for gold.

"I'll be going then and thank you," I says, standing up and turning to leave.

"Give Marilyn a little kiss on your way out," Carrigan says.

"I got a wife," I says.

"So have I. I got a wife for fifty years and I love her dearly."

"I got a wife who's having a baby."

His expression changes. It gets soft. "Ah, that's another thing altogether."

When I step off the elevator down in the lobby I almost bump into Marilyn and the poodle, both of which are looking like they been blown around by the wind a little, except Marilyn's got a worried look on her face and Mistinguette's got a satisfied look on hers.

"You look upset," I says.

"When I got out to the street with Mistinguette there was a mangy mutt tied to the fire hydrant. He takes one look at Mistinguette and busts the leash."

"Oh, dear," I says, "she ain't in heat, I hope."

"Well, if she is, she just started. Even so, that damned mongrel had his way with her."

I thought that sounded like a pretty Victorian way for a Chicago girl to talk but I don't mention it.

"It was all the cop could do to drag him off her."

"Cop?"

"One was passing by in a squad car. He saw that Mistinguette was in some distress."

And probably saw your skirt blowing up around your buns, I thought.

"Let's hope no harm done," I says, hoping that I don't get the answer I'm afraid I could get to my next question. "Did the cop take the mutt away with him?"

"It got away. Went running off down the street and the officer took off after it in his car, so I don't know."

I give Mistinguette a pat on the head and Marilyn a quick smile, then I'm out of there.

I give a look around and there comes Alfie out of an alley, dragging his leash behind him, looking like the cat that got the canary, or putting it right on the line, the mutt that got to the poodle.

I open the car door quick and Alfie jumps right in.

I go around and get behind the wheel. "Keep your head down," I says. "That cop could still be around."

Alfie ducks down, still grinning. I'm grinning, too, figuring we got away clean. Then I look into the rearview and there's Marilyn and Mistinguette standing on the sidewalk, looking our way. I think she saw me with the villain what done it.

• 3 •

"HOW DID YOU DO with Ray Carrigan?" Mike asks me. It's Tuesday night and my father always comes over for stew and Irish soda bread on Tuesday nights. He comes for supper other nights, too, but Tuesday nights he never misses.

"He said he'd think about it," I says.

"Is that all he said?"

"He told me to give his receptionist a kiss on the way out."

"What?" Mary says, standing at the stove giving the stew a last shake of salt and pepper.

"That's a good sign," Mike says. "It means he's favorably disposed toward you and the request you made of him."

"Wait a minute, wait a minute," Mary says, facing both of us like she's ready to start a fight. "Run that train by me one more time. I think I missed it."

The thought comes to me that Mary's starting to talk

like Mike and me and I ain't sure that's such a good thing.

"Carrigan's got his little ways," Mike says. "He likes to make people squirm."

"And toss pretty women at my husband's head?"

"He used to throw Goldie at you in the old days. You could think he was offering you romance but you'd be wrong," Mike says, the mention of Goldie clearly bringing back good memories.

I give him the old one-eye, wondering if maybe there was a little something going on there sometime along the way. But Mike won't look at me so I figure I'll just have to keep on wondering.

"What did this receptionist you were supposed to kiss look like?" Mary asks, dishing out the stew.

"Well, she has red hair . . ." I start to say.

Mary throws the ladle into the pot, puts the soup bowl on the stove, and runs out of the kitchen.

"Now you done it," Mike says.

"What did I do?"

"Told Mary that Carrigan's receptionist was a pretty redhead."

"I didn't even say she was pretty."

"To a woman a redhead's got to be pretty."

"I see plenty of homely redheads."

"To a pregnant woman a pretty redhead's a threat to her marriage."

"Maybe to some pregnant women, but Mary's a nurse."

"What's that supposed to mean?"

"Well, it means that a nurse knows about things like the funny ideas women get when they get pregnant. It's the hormones."

"You got to understand something, Jim, Mary's not a nurse every minute. She's not even the wife you knew.

She's a pregnant mother-to-be and not responsible for her feelings or her actions."

"Don't let Mary or any of her friends hear you say that or we'll have a fight on our hands that'll last a year. So what are we supposed to do now?"

Mike reaches over for the bowl of stew Mary already dished out.

"I'm going to eat my supper," he says, "but if I was you I'd go into the bedroom and try to make it up with Mary."

I go in and find her laying facedown on the bed. I start to say something nice but she tells me to go eat my supper and leave her alone. So that's what I do.

We're laying in bed around eleven o'clock, awake but not saying anything. Mary's curled up on her side, pretending to be asleep, and I'm laying on my back staring up at the ceiling thinking about pregnancy, wondering if I'm really glad that Mary's in the family way and worrying that maybe Mistinguette is, too.

How long I wonder does it take before you can tell if a dog's pregnant?

Mary turns over onto her back. Then she rolls over toward me and throws her arm over my chest.

"I'm sorry, James," she says. She's practically the only person what calls me James ever since my mother—God bless and keep her—died.

"You got nothing to be sorry for," I says.

"I'm sorry I blew up like that."

"It wasn't so bad."

"I hope I didn't upset Mike."

"You didn't upset him much. He had two bowls of stew and half a loaf of bread."

"I hope I didn't hurt your feelings."

"Well, no, but you had me confused there. I just told

you what Carrigan said to do to his receptionist. I didn't say I did it."

"Did you want to do it?"

"It never entered my mind."

"You're a very attractive man, do you know that, James?"

"Some people say I look like Jimmy Cagney when he was Yankee Doodle Dandy," I says, kidding right along.

"That was a good old picture."

"So if a person thinks that Jimmy Cagney was good-looking in *Yankee Doodle Dandy*, then maybe they'd think I was good-looking," I says.

"You're better looking than Jimmy Cagney in *Yankee Doodle Dandy*," Mary says, nuzzling her nose into my neck. "You're as good-looking as Jimmy Cagney was in *The Strawberry Blonde*."

"I never saw that one."

"I've seen bits and pieces on the graveyard shift at Passavant."

"I didn't kiss Carrigan's receptionist," I says, "but there's a chance Alfie did that and even worse to Carrigan's dog."

"What do you mean Alfie did something worse?"

"You know."

"Show me," she says.

After a while Mary says, "Hell, you go tell Carrigan's dog what Alfie did wasn't so bad." Then she snuggles down and falls asleep.

The phone rings four or five times around six o'clock in the morning. I let it ring and Mary don't wake up.

Around eight o'clock it rings again. I trot out into the kitchen in my bare feet. The linoleum's cold. Alfie looks up at me from his bed.

"Hello?" I says.

"Flannery?" the phone says.

"It's me," I says. "Who's this?"

"I want you to come over to Saganashkee Slough by the dam which is at the west end."

Now that I got more than one word I recognize the voice. It's Carrigan on the phone. For a minute I have the crazy thought that he's going to tell me he knows all about Alfie and his poodle.

"I don't know this Saganashkee Slough," I says.

He blows air through his nose like he can't understand a man what has lived in Chicago more than two years who don't know where is Saganashkee Slough. "You take Stevenson to Kingery Highway, south to a Hundred and seventh Street and go east about three miles. The dam'll be off to your right. I'll have a county car waiting on the road and somebody in it to walk you down to the equestrian trail."

"Somebody we know get hisself hurt riding a horse?" I says.

"Somebody got herself killed."

I wait a second. It ain't long in coming.

"Goldie Hanrahan's dead."

• 4 •

SAGANASHKEE SLOUGH is a forest preserve next to Palos Hills. The Cook County cop is waiting on the shoulder of 107th. I pull in behind him and park.

When I get out and open the door for Alfie, the cop says, "That your tracker?" and gives a laugh what sounds like a snort.

"Well, I guess he could do that if I asked him," I says.

"So you better put him on a lead where we're going. We don't want him rooting around where he don't belong."

I put Alfie on the leash, which don't seem to bother him much though he gives me a look like he's saying I should know better than to think he'd misbehave.

We follow the cop down the trail to the dam. There's a horse trail that goes along the edge of the slough, well back among the underbrush and trees. There's a couple of jeeps and a safari wagon parked in a clearing and a bunch of people gathered in one spot.

Two kids about twelve, thirteen, are standing in front

of a big deputy on a little hill of grass off to one side. One of them looks like Tom Sawyer and the other one like Huck Finn. I figure they were the ones found Goldie, but what they were doing around Saganashkee Slough that hour of the morning is anybody's guess.

I see Carrigan among them. He's dressed like he's going to a wedding or a funeral. He's wearing a dark topcoat with a velvet collar and he's got a white scarf around his neck. Also he's wearing a homburg, which looks very strange out in the woods especially since everybody else is in down vests or plaid flannel shirts and boots. He's looking at something on the ground.

A big cop in a leather jacket is standing next to him. He ain't wearing the standard holster and belt. Instead he's got a pearl-handled revolver in a holster riding low on his leg and tied down like he's some old-style western gunfighter. It's Koslow, the sheriff of Cook County. He's looking at the ground, too.

He turns around and looks past my escort at me. Then Carrigan looks.

Nobody greets me. We just shake hands all around, then all three of us look down at the woman laying in the dirt and leaves.

Sidney Hackman, the medical examiner, is down on one knee doing a gross examination of Goldie Hanrahan's body.

When he stands up I get a good look at all of her. I'd just as soon I didn't. Her face has been all smashed in and her teeth knocked out.

"Horse run away on her?" I asks.

"That what you think done it?" Carrigan says.

Koslow gives him a look like, there you are, you wanted this sewer inspector called to the scene like he could do what trained officers of the law can't be expected to do, so what happens? He comes to the same conclusion we come to.

"I didn't say that, but there she is with her face smashed in and there's a bloody limb off a tree not ten feet away and I don't see a horse, so I'm asking the first question that comes to mind seeing all those things."

"So where's her bridgework?" Carrigan says.

"Well, I didn't get that close a look. Is her bridgework missing?"

"It wasn't knocked down her throat," Hackman says. "At least not so far as I can tell before I open her up."

"You mean she could've swallowed her teeth?"

"It's possible. You'd be surprised the things that're possible when it comes to violent death."

"So we can't count out misadventure until you have a look, right?"

Everybody's eyebrows go up when I say "misadventure," like just because a man's a little careless with grammar, what with his background, upbringing, and all, he's dumb and wouldn't know such a word.

"She was raped," Carrigan says.

I take another look. This time I'm not looking at the horrible sight which is her face. This time I see that her belt's been undone and the fly unbuttoned.

"I didn't say rape," Hackman corrects him. "I said it looks like she'd been interfered with."

"But you won't know until you open her up," Carrigan says with a sarcastic edge to it.

Hackman dead-eyes him. "Well, at least until I've had a look. I don't go around deciding things until I've had a look."

"It doesn't look to me that we're doing Goldie one damn bit of good standing here asking was she raped, wasn't she raped, did she swallow her teeth, didn't she swallow her teeth," Carrigan says.

Nobody says whatever we do ain't going to do Goldie any good anymore because we all know that what Carrigan is talking about is payback. Revenge. If somebody or something killed his old friend, somebody or something was going to have to pay for it. If it ended up her horse ran her into a tree, Carrigan would see to it that the horse was shot and the tree chopped down and burned.

"So what do you think?" Carrigan asks, looking right at me.

I really don't know what I'm supposed to say or do.

"I don't know how you work it in the city," Koslow growls, "but in the county the sheriff's office handles investigations."

Carrigan looks up into Koslow's face, the funny thing being that he's much shorter but it still looks like he's dominating the bigger man. "Flannery's my personal representative in this, Stanislaus. It's like he's representing the Democratic Party, if you get my meaning."

"I'm just saying we don't mind if he tags along but I'm giving him fair warning. He interferes with the progress of our investigation, we'll put him someplace where he won't bother us."

Here I am called in at the crack of dawn to look at an ugly sight and already I'm being told what to do by Carrigan—who was jerking my chain, teasing me about the committeeman's spot just the day before—and getting threatened by the sheriff of Cook County.

"All right if I call you later, Sidney?" Carrigan asks Hackman.

"It'll be a couple of days. We're crowded."

Carrigan clears his throat.

"Try me tonight, right after supper," Hackman says. "But no promises."

"Those two kids over there have anything to do with this?" I asks.

"They found the body," Koslow says.

"What time was that?"

"Just after it got light."

"What was they doing out around here that hour of the morning?"

"They say they were camping out."

"Is that what they say? What about school?"

"Well they told me they got the day before Thanksgiving and the day after Thanksgiving."

"That's right. Tomorrow's Thanksgiving, ain't it? I almost forgot. So them two is just kids playing Pilgrims and Indians, huh?"

"They look like a pair of killers to you, Flannery?" Koslow says, the sarcasm thick as a slab of cheese on a working man's sandwich.

The hell with it, I think. "I'll just go on over there and have a talk with them."

"I can't have you interfering with witnesses," Koslow says.

Carrigan clears his throat.

Koslow raises his hand and hooks his finger at the big deputy. When he starts to move away from the kids without bringing them along, Koslow says, "Bring them two with you."

The deputy wraps each hand around an arm of one of the two kids and escorts them down to us like they was in custody.

"Be careful," Koslow tells me. "These kids are scared and we don't want them telling their parents the police scared them more."

"I'm not the police."

"They don't know that."

"I'll tell them," I says as the kids come to a stop in

front of us. One kid's got the map of Ireland on his kisser—pale red, almost orange hair, blue eyes, freckles, buck teeth, and a turned-up nose. The whole look. The other one's Puerto Rican, maybe Mexican.

"My name's Jimmy Flannery," I says. "I ain't a cop."

The Irish kid grins at me.

"What's your names?" I goes on.

"I'm Patrick Behan and my friend here's Julio Banda," Pat pipes up, respectful as you please, giving me a five-buck grin. Julio just stands there looking wide-eyed and solemn.

"You found the lady?" I asks.

"Yessir, we did," Pat says.

I never see such an innocent face. His friend, Julio, ain't doing as good. He's letting Pat do the talking because I figure he don't trust his voice.

"What time was that?" I asks.

Pat shrugs. "I'm sorry to say I don't know exactly, sir. I ain't got a watch. But it was light."

"You hear her fall?"

"We heard something, sir. It woke us up."

"Where was you?"

"Over there." He points out past the trail and the stand of trees to the edge of Saganashkee Slough beyond.

"What was the sound like?"

"Don't know. We was asleep and it woke us up."

"So that was it? Some noise woke you up but it didn't register what caused it?"

"Yessir."

"There wasn't any more noise?"

"We heard a woman scream again."

"That what woke you up? Her screaming the first time?"

"I don't understand, mister. What do you mean the first time?"

"You said you heard a woman scream again, so that must mean you heard her scream twice."

"I never thought about it but I guess that's the way it was. That the way it was, Julio?"

Julio nods his head like he's afraid if he does it too hard it'll fall off.

"So what else did you hear?"

"Hoofbeats, like in the movies."

"The horse running away?"

"I guess."

"Then what did you do after the noise woke you up and you heard a woman scream and a horse run away?"

"We came out of the trees over there. At first we didn't see nothing and then Julio saw the lady's shirt."

"Her sleeve," Julio says, speaking up for the first time, his voice like a rusty hinge. He's got a little accent. He gives you the feeling he don't speak very much, only when he has to. "It was white."

"That's right," Pat says, smiling at his friend like he's proud of him, like he invented him or like he's doing things right for a change. "Then we see her laying there dead."

"How did you know she was dead?"

"You could see she wasn't breathing."

"You got that close?"

"Sure," he says, boasting a little about how brave he is.

"You touch her?"

"Noooo," he says, backing off as though that was asking too much even from a brave guy like him.

Julio backs off, too, wanting no part of any conversation about touching a dead person.

"Where'd you go to report it?"

"Up onto a Hundred and seventh," Pat says. "That right, Julio?"

"I had to walk back almost to Archer before a car come along and stopped for me," Julio says.

"You went by yourself?"

He nods and Pat says, like he's very proud of hisself, "I stayed with the victim."

"After you called the police what'd you do, Julio?"

"I waited at the gas station where I made the call until the sheriffs come and got me."

"How long was you gone altogether?"

"I don't know." His eyes flicker toward Pat like he's hoping for some instructions. But Pat's just smiling like the angel on a wedding cake. "Maybe an hour. Maybe more."

"We got the call at seven twenty-two," Koslow says.

"About fifteen minutes from the road to here," I says, thinking out loud. "How long you wait for a ride?"

"Ten, fifteen minutes."

Julio's starting to look distressed, like so much talking's starting to get him down.

"Five minutes, maybe ten, to the gas station," I goes on, "so Goldie got killed between say six-twenty and six thirty-five, give or take."

I look down at the ground like I'm thinking. I look up at Pat from under my eyebrows. He's as cool as a pig on ice.

"While you was here alone with the body, what was you doing, Pat?"

"I was just sitting down over there guarding the poor woman," he says. "There's animals in these woods, you know."

"Okay, that's enough," Koslow says.

He jerks his chin at the deputy, who puts his meat hooks on their arms again.

"Hey, what's going on?" Pat demands. "Where you taking us?"

"Taking you into headquarters to get your statements. Then taking you home. Anything wrong with that?"

"Well, Jesus, ain't there no reward?"

"Your reward's the good feeling you get for doing your duty as a citizen," Koslow says.

I go into my pocket and look at what I got in my money clip. It ain't much but I peel off two fives and give one to each kid.

"Hey," Koslow says.

"They could be getting hungry. That's so they can buy some breakfast."

"I was going to see they got some breakfast," Koslow said, a bundle of injured feelings.

"Hey, now wait," Pat pipes up again, pulling against the deputy's grip. "We'd just as soon you didn't tell our parents nothing about this."

"How's that?" Koslow says. "You supposed to be in school?"

"We just thought we'd take the extra day," Pat says.

"Well, ain't your folks going to wonder where you been all night?" I asks.

"Julio's ma and pa think he's at my house and my ma and pa think I'm over to his house. You going to get us in trouble? Is that what we're going to get for being good citizens?"

It was a pleasure to see and hear the kid work his marks.

"Don't give me any trouble and we'll see what we'll see," Koslow says.

"Well, that's all I can do here," I says, and start walking away, tapping Carrigan on the elbow as I pass him.

He follows me along the trail a little way to where I can cut through on up to the road the way I came.

"What is it?" Carrigan says.

"I'm asking you, Mr. Carrigan," I says. "Just what am I supposed to be doing around here?"

"Looking out for my interests, Jimmy," he says, staring at me, "just like I'm always happy to look out for yours. I don't know what the sheriff'll turn up, or what you'll turn up, but I'm sure that whatever you turn up'll get back to me before it gets to the sheriffs or the cops."

"If I find out anything they should know I'll have to tell them. You understand that?"

"I wouldn't want you to do anything you couldn't live with."

"That's all I'm saying."

"Well, then, that settles that. We'll just have to see what we'll see and take our chances. Just so long as we've taken every reasonable precaution," Carrigan adds, the way the best politicians put in the zinger, "to make sure that justice is done."

I start into the trees along the footpath.

"Where are you going, Flannery?" Carrigan says.

"To see a man about a horse."

• 5 •

I DON'T NEED A MAP to get around Chicago but I'm over west of the Tri-State Tollway so I got to go to my book of maps and my Yellow Pages, which I always keep in the trunk of my car.

There's not a hell of a lot of stables in greater Chicago, maybe two dozen. Goldie lives—lived—out around Artesian and Seventy-first near Marquette Park in the Fifteenth Ward. The closest stables are on Kean alongside the forest preserve. She wants to go for a ride she could drive about three and a half miles south on Western, then west about nine miles on Ninety-fifth. Most times of the day figure about twenty minutes tops.

It's six of one, half a dozen the other, which stable, Hickory Boarding Farms or Hilltop Stables, is closest. I go to the one in Hickory Hills first, figuring I got a fifty-fifty chance to be right first shot and get there before Koslow sends somebody out to ask the same questions I'm going to ask.

The man what comes toddling out from under a big

chestnut tree has a belly on him like a pregnant sow, though a pregnant sow is nothing I ever saw or am even likely to see.

"Call me Fats," he says, and sticks out his hand. "Nice dog you got there. What kind is he?"

"Never thought to ask."

"Probably a Heinzhound," he says, grinning like he loved Alfie and me and the smell of horseshit in the air.

"How's that?"

"Fifty-seven varieties," he says. "Get it?"

When he sees I'm still puzzled he says, "You're probably too young to remember," but the passing of time and the way his joke falls flat don't bother Fats for more than a second. "What can I do you for?"

"Did a lady by the name of Hanrahan rent a horse from you this morning?"

"Nosir."

"Thanks anyway," I says, and start to walk back to my car.

"Hold it," Fats said. "You didn't tell me your name."

"It's Jimmy Flannery."

"Not the same Jimmy Flannery what found a body chewed in half down in the sewers? Not the same Flannery what arrested that photographer what killed that pretty model? Not the Flannery what—"

"How come you remember all that stuff?" I says, interrupting him before he goes on to tell me the story of my life.

"I read the papers, don't I? I got nothing to do all day but sit in the shade and read the newspapers, don't I?"

"How about taking care of the horses?"

"I got stable hands to do that."

"Well, I'm pleased to meet you, Fats," I says, and start to go on my way again.

"Hold it," he says. "You asked me did this lady,

Hanrahan, rent a horse. I said, no, she didn't rent a horse. You didn't ask me did I board a horse for her."

"Do you?"

"Yes, I do."

"Could I see it?"

"You're sure you're Jimmy Flannery?"

"I could show you credentials."

He waves the suggestion away and says, "This way."

I follow his waddle down the yard, under the chestnut tree, around the corner of a barn, and down a long line of box stalls with a training ring in the distance down at the other end.

"What the hell," Fats says when we get about midway and he stops at a stall with a half-opened door top and bottom. "Well, that's all right, then. For a minute I thought somebody'd stole Tea."

"Tea?"

"That's Goldie Hanrahan's mare. But there she is standing in her stall as quiet as you please."

"She don't look all that quiet to me," I says. "You think that's because she's wearing a saddle?"

"I'll be damned," Fats says, and goes in to scratch the mare on the jaw and look into her eye. "She's been scared and on the run," he adds, running his hand down her shoulder then putting it to his nose. "You ready to tell me what's going on?"

"Goldie Hanrahan was found on one of the trails up at the end of Saganashkee Slough. Her face was smashed by a tree limb. She's dead."

He stands there for a long minute like he's stunned. "I can't hardly believe it."

"I know. She was a friend of mine, too. You never expect something like that to happen to a friend."

"It must've been something terrible to scare Tea enough to have her run off on Goldie. She's the steadiest mount I see in years."

"Would she just keep on running after Goldie left the saddle?"

"There's no telling what a horse—any animal—might do given this situation or that."

"She might have bolted and Goldie got knocked off or . . . ?"

"Or Goldie got knocked off and then Tea came on home. Now *that* you can figure just about any horse'll do. She's been boarded here better'n three years and knows her way from any place out in the preserve."

"So we've got a case of misadventure or a crime," I says.

"Which one are you betting on?"

"How often did Goldie ride?"

"Weekends generally. Saturday and Sunday. Sometimes on a Friday or a Monday. Also whenever she wanted to get away and think things out. That's what she told me."

"What time of day?"

He shrugs his shoulders, which I take to mean no special time or whenever the spirit moved her.

"Before six A.M.?"

Fats shook his head. "I'd say that'd be unusual."

"Where'd she usually ride? She ever say?"

"She'd take Tea along the trails to Bellydeep, then around the bottom and over to Cranberry, then up around the top of Buttonbush and down around Redwing before coming home. Them is all sloughs."

"She go out to Saganashkee Slough very often?"

"I suppose she's been everywhere in the preserve but I don't know as how she made a point of going out to Saganashkee much."

"How far is it out to the western edge of Saganashkee Slough from here?"

"Well, as the crow flies, about four miles. But being as how we ain't crows it'd more likely be eight or nine."

"How long'd that take on horseback?"

"Depends was you walking, trotting, or going at a canter—nobody'd want to gallop those trails for any distance—say an hour and a half, two hours."

"According to the map, anybody who drove from here to where she was found would only have to travel about five and a half miles down along Kean and over a Hundred and seventh."

"That sounds right."

"Six, seven minutes by car against an hour and a half on horseback."

"You puzzling something out?" Fats says, cocking his head like a bird eyeing a bug, really interested in what he thinks is a detective working it out.

"Could I find my way over to Saganashkee Slough on my own?" I asks.

"What for?"

"See if I can trace the route she took."

"What then?"

"I might find something along the way."

"Like what?"

"I ain't got the vaguest idea."

"You good in the woods?"

"I don't spend a lot of time in them."

"So I better go along and see if I can be any help."

"That's kind of you," I says.

He shrugs and even colors a little like compliments embarrass him.

"Let's get a couple of horses out here, then," he says. "What do you ride?"

"How's that?"

"You ride English or you ride Western?"

"I don't ride neither."

"You ever been on a horse?"

"My dad put me up on a pony once to have my picture taken."

"Maude'll do for you."

He steps over to the next stall and slips a rope halter over the nose of a horse that looks to be about the tallest horse I ever see. It's a lean and lanky mare with sleepy eyes who looks at me like she can't understand why I should be bothering her in the middle of the morning.

"Just take this rope while I get a horse for myself and we'll walk on down to the corral and saddle 'em up," Fats says.

"Ain't you got something shorter?"

"Well, here's the way I figure, Mr. Flannery. You want to learn how to ride a horse, ride a tall horse. Fall off a tall horse and you'll see to it you never fall off again."

We walk on a ways, me leading Maude, until Fats stops at another stall and brings out a horse that's as big around as he is, comparing horse to man.

We go on down to the corral. I watch as Fats and the stable hand throw on the blankets and saddles and cinch them up. Fats tells the hand where we're going and the hand just grunts and offers Maude the bit. She don't want to take it at first but he slaps her on the neck and she says okay. Finally we're ready to go.

Fats lifts his leg, sticks his boot in the stirrup, and lifts hisself into the saddle slick as a whistle. It's a big struggle for me to climb up the side of that lanky horse, Fats giving me the old one-eye all the time but being too polite to laugh.

Alfie's too polite to give me the ha-ha, too. Besides, this could be the first time he's ever seen a horse and he's not too sure what he's got to deal with here.

So we start off at a slow walk with Fats in front, me on Maude in the middle, and Alfie, staying well away from Maude's hooves, bringing up the rear.

By the time we get to Bellydeep Slough I'm feeling it

inside my thighs. We trot for a couple of miles through the forest but the pounding of my rump on the saddle gets to be more than I can handle so we do the rest of it to Saganashkee Slough at a walk, me looking right and left along the trail and down at the dirt and leaves in front of me, trying to pick up any clues that could be laying along the way.

I start wondering what the hell I expect to find along eight or nine miles of trails covered in forest rubble, but it's too late to turn back so I just keep on plodding along, looking at the ground and looking at the two broad backsides in front of me.

Every once in a while Fats points a finger at a clod of dirt kicked aside by a passing hoof or a broken twig still showing green. "Rider passed by here this morning," he says every time.

Twice we pass ragged-looking men, one with a beard, one without, carrying duffels on their shoulders. They step aside and let us pass, looking up at us sideways. Another time we hear some crashing in the brush alongside the trail.

"Animal?" I asks.

"More likely another one of them vagrants we passed," Fats says.

"There many of them in the woods?"

"Some. No way to make a living or the price of a pint in the preserve, but there's some that'd rather spend the night sleeping in the windbreak of a stand of trees than in some city gutter or doorway. They come out at night."

"Who'd give them a ride if they was hitching?"

Fats shrugs. "People'll find a way to get to some comfort if they can."

"You ever see any homeless? Any women or children?"

"Oh, yes. The rangers gather 'em up. Take 'em back to shelters if they can find one. Mostly women. Women on their own ain't as good at ducking the law as the men."

"How about the kids?"

"Oh, they get along. They're small so they can hide and find places that a grown person'd just walk on by."

"You see any kids around lately?"

"Oh, sure."

"A redhead by the name of Pat and his sidekick, a Latino by the name of Julio?"

"I don't know what their names was, but a couple of kids fit that description came by last week looking for work. Spending money they said, like they was just a couple of locals looking for a little something to do after school. But they was runaways."

"You give them anything to do?"

"Didn't have anything. Besides, you let kids like that much around horses and the first thing you know you got an injury and that could mean trouble, one way or another."

"When was the last you seen them?"

"Maybe it was Saturday."

I got nothing else to ask. I just ride along hoping that Koslow don't let those two kids get away on us.

It's warming up the closer we get to Saganashkee Slough and I can smell the rotting vegetation of the wetlands. They smell a lot like a funeral parlor.

"There any snakes around here?" I asks.

Fats lifts his head a little so his voice will carry back to me without him having to turn around and says, "Some copperheads. Cottonmouth. Rattler here and there, maybe. Garden snakes and black snakes. A lot of them. Saw a king snake more than once or twice. Why you ask?"

"I seem to remember reading once that horses are crazy scared of snakes."

"Some are. Some aren't. Like anything else, what people say ain't always the truth."

A breeze blows up across a little clearing alongside the trail and kicks up a flurry of leaves, which makes Maude skitter and sidestep, nearly jogging me out of the saddle. I let out a yell but I hold on. Fats wheels his big horse around to see what I'm doing.

"See there?" he says. "It's like I say. Maude's steady as a rock, but that little wind upset her. Can never tell with horses."

I'm really glad to get to the spot where Goldie's body'd been found. I expect to see some mobile-lab people wearing rubber gloves, their pockets full of glassine bags, crawling around the underbrush on their hands and knees, but there's nobody around. The scene looks undisturbed. They ain't even taped out the outline of her body the way you see them do on television.

Fats looks disappointed, too, like he's been hoping for something more than a rough patch of ground among a million other rough patches of ground.

I get down off Maude, my legs nearly giving way under me, and start walking here and there, peering down like a bird looking for a worm.

Fats dismounts but stands in one place like he's afraid he'll spoil evidence if he moves.

After about ten minutes he says, "Finding anything?" practically in a whisper.

"Fats," I says, "I got to tell you the truth. I don't know what the hell we're doing here. It seemed like a good idea back at the stables. Now I can't imagine why I took the trip. Maybe I expected to find something that'd say to me that her horse ran away on her, or somebody jumped out at her and dragged her out of the saddle, or whatever. Maybe I expected to get lucky and have her teeth jump up and bite me." I was sorry that popped out right after I said it. "But I don't see a damn thing that answers any of my questions," I finished up, feeling pretty lame and useless.

"Like what?"

"Like did Goldie come out here to meet somebody, or, if there was an assailant, was he another early-morning rider or a vagrant like the ones we saw, who just happened to see her? And if she was meeting somebody here, how come she rode horseback eight or nine miles instead of driving five and a half in the comfort of a car?"

"I hear what you're saying."

"Most of all, this minute, I'd like to know how come there ain't a bunch of sheriff's men and lab technicians going over this ground looking for whatever."

"How's that?" Fats says.

"Well, you got to figure if there's a reason for people to do this or that, there's got to be a reason why they don't do this or that. Like somebody don't want to do this or that or have it done."

"Or sometimes things just don't get done or fall through the cracks or people slip up," Fats says, and I can't say no to that.

• 6 •

THERE'S NOTHING MORE I can see to do around Saganashkee Slough, so it looks like it's time to climb back up into the saddle, which is something I'm not looking forward to. I got my leg raised when we hear the motor of a four-wheeler grinding and groaning toward us.

"Motor vehicles not allowed on these trails," Fats says.

"Well, let's just see who it is," I says, having a pretty good idea of who it could be.

Sure enough, when the jeep comes into sight along the trail that goes up to 107th, a deputy's driving and Koslow's riding alongside him. The tires spurt dirt as the driver brakes and turns the wheel, sending the jeep into a little skid like a horse pulling up to the saloon in a western movie. Koslow seems pleased with the perform-ance.

He steps down and strides over to me, hitching up his

gun belt with the pearl-handled forty-five like we was going to have it out right then and there.

"I thought I gave you the word," he says.

"What word is that?" I says.

"That you was supposed to keep your nose out of this situation and leave it up to me."

"Leave what up to you?"

"The situation concerning Goldie Hanrahan."

"Well, what's the situation about Goldie Hanrahan?"

"We don't know yet, do we? Probably an accident. Horse bolted on her. That's how it looks to me."

When I don't say anything he goes on, "Is that how it still looks to you?"

"I don't know. I don't think I'll be able to make up my mind until I find out what Hackman has to say about was she molested, about did she swallow her bridgework."

"Me, too. That's what I'm waiting for, too."

"How come you ain't got any men out here beating the bushes?"

He don't answer me.

"How come you ain't got even a deputy posted? Anyone could come along, trample all over evidence. Maybe even find the missing teeth, pick them up, put them in a pocket, and walk away with them."

He gives me the old one-eye and jerks his thumb at the deputy standing there. "What do think I come back with him for?"

"It's a little late, wouldn't you say?"

"Except for you there isn't a lot of traffic around here, would you say? I had things to look into and I wanted Sheldon along."

"Sheldon?"

"My deputy here."

"What things was you looking into?"

"Like where her horse come from and where it went."

"Looks like we had the same idea," I says, giving him the old buddy-buddy grin.

"I found that out, didn't I, when I went over to Hickory Hills and had a talk with the stable hand." He looks at Fats, who's standing there calm and easy, a man who knows there's no suspicion coming his way. "You the boss of Hickory Hills?"

"Fats Coolidge," Fats says, like Koslow'd asked him his name.

"You two disturb anything around here?"

"I been standing and looking," Fats says.

"Nothing to disturb," I says. "Nobody watching the area. It ain't even marked off as a crime scene."

"We already had our discussion about that. Besides, we don't know it's a crime scene," Koslow says.

I can see we're going to start going around in circles, so I shrug my shoulders and clam up.

"Why don't you go back to the city, Flannery?" Koslow says. "You don't look happy."

"Well, I'm not happy, Sheriff. My friend Ray Carrigan, the Democratic Party leader, asked me to look into this situation. I'd just as soon not. But he asked me as a friend and I don't know what else to do. I don't want to get in anybody's way."

"You can get into anybody's way you want just so long as you don't get into mine," Koslow says.

"I'll see to that," I says.

"Then we got an understanding?"

"I'd say so."

He finally gives me a smile, figuring he's won. What he don't know is I already decided the answer to what happened to Goldie ain't in the woods but right back there in Chicago.

"Any chance you could drive me back to Hickory Farms in the jeep?" I says.

He hesitates a moment.

"Like you say, I ain't really comfortable out here and I sure ain't comfortable on a horse. That okay with you, Fats?"

Fats gives me a grin and a wave.

"So, how about it, Sheriff?"

Koslow's overflowing with the milk of human kindness so he says, "Get in."

I get in the back. Alfie jumps onto the seat beside me. Koslow gets behind the wheel, cranks her up, and pops the clutch so hard the jeep bucks out like a horse what was spurred.

• 7 •

WHEN ALFIE AND ME get home, Mary's got a shopping list for me. I go up to Mr. Panatone, the butcher, to see if the bird I ordered last week is waiting for me, which it is. Also I get the sausage for the dressing.

I go over to the liquor store for some wine. I don't drink it but Mike and Mary's mother, Charlotte, and her aunt Sada like a glass on a special occasion. So does Mary. Mike's bringing sweet cider for me. One of his friends at the firehouse brings it down from his place at the lake, which is close to a cider mill that's started up again to serve the gourmet trade. There's always a way to get something a little special.

I get two loaves of day-old bread from the bake shop for the stuffing. Charlotte and Sada are bringing the pies.

Most of the groceries—the potatoes, pearl onions, turnips, green beans, celery, cans of black olives, cranberry sauce and consommé, sweet potatoes and mushrooms—I get right downstairs in the grocery store owned and run by Joe and Pearl Pakula.

I stop along the way for a bunch of flowers and a box of thin mints for after dinner, which ain't on the list but which is totally my own idea.

Mary's sitting in the kitchen by the window in a patch of sun that falls like butter on the tablecloth. It's picking out the red glints in her hair. Her eyes look like she's a million miles away; she didn't even hear me let myself in the front door. I stand there with my arms full of groceries while Alfie trots over and sits by her leg. He pushes his nose into her lap where her hands are folded one on top of the other, palms up, like she's holding something small against her belly. She's not showing yet but I know she's cradling the baby that's growing in there. Alfie pushes against her wrist with his nose.

She pats his head and turns her head real slow to look down into his face. Then she raises her eyes to me.

My heart pushes against my chest. I can hardly breathe and I know when people talk about loving someone so much it hurts.

"You got everything you went for?" she asks.

"I think I did," I says, "but a dime'll get you a dollar I forgot something."

"It won't matter," she says.

I put the bags on the counter near the stove. I go over and get down on my knees by her.

"I got to stick my nose in your lap to get a hug and a pat?" I says.

She kisses me.

Tomorrow's Thanksgiving.

It's my favorite holiday.

• 8 •

I WONDER what people did to celebrate the good things in life before there was a Thanksgiving Day in America. I know they had harvest festivals in Europe, Africa, and Asia. I read once about the harvest celebrations in the Euphrates Valley when I was a kid in grammar school.

But how could it be the same without turkey and cranberry sauce and stuffing and mashed potatoes with gravy?

Anyway, the way a house smells on Thanksgiving Day gives me the warmest feeling, but I told Mary, seeing as how she was pregnant and cooking a dinner like that ain't easy, I'd take her and my old man and her mother and her aunt out to dinner at some restaurant.

"Dan Blatna's Sold Out Saloon over to the Thirty-second Ward, which is famous for their kielbasas and cabbage, puts on an old-fashioned American feast, the only difference being they use Polish sausage in the dressing."

But Mary won't have restaurants for Thanksgiving

dinner, and "besides," she says, "my mother and my aunt Sada want to help. "Also Janet"—Canarias, the alderwoman—"and your friend Willy Dink"—the non-polluting, all-natural pest exterminator—"are invited. Not to mention your father."

I'm very glad Mary refuses the offer.

Charlotte and Sada arrive first thing in the morning with the pies: pumpkin, apple, and mince.

Mike gets there an hour later with two jugs of cider. One sweet and the other hard, because he always keeps one from last year's pressing, which sits all year in a dark closet building up a little kick. He won't drink the pasteurized cider you buy in the stores.

By the time the cooking gets under way Mike and me've got a choice. We can sit in the parlor and watch the football games or we can go up on the roof and get the sun, which is still very warm, considering it's the beginning of winter, or we can take a walk around the neighborhood to see if there's anybody needs any help on a day when everybody else's got it pretty good.

So first we stop into the grocery store downstairs and ask Joe and Pearl Pakula—who keep open until noon in case there's anybody forgot a quart of milk, a loaf of bread, this or that—is there anybody they heard of who ain't got the fixings for a Thanksgiving dinner, but Joe and Pearl say they ain't heard of nobody, which they would've if the churches and charities, the Democratic Party and me, ain't made sure everybody who needs one has a basket.

"You know," Mike says, after we leave the grocery store and go walking around giving a wave and a smile to everybody we meet and passing the time of day with anyone who wants to chew the fat, "no matter how bad things go the rest of the year, it hurts twice as bad if a person ain't got the makings of a Thanksgiving dinner

on Thanksgiving and a little Christmas cheer on Christmas. Good things seems a little better and bad things a
lot sadder around them two days. Like Goldie getting
killed the way she did. I been thinking about her since I
got up this morning."

"You know her pretty good?" I asks.

"What do you mean by pretty good?" Mike asks back.

"Well, I mean you was at all the Democratic fund-
raisers for forty years. You was a precinct captain for
thirty-five. You must've broke bread with Ray Carrigan
a hundred times. And anybody who broke bread with
Carrigan or even asked a favor had to meet Goldie."

"Oh, I met her," Mike says.

"What kind of a woman was she?"

"She was a pretty woman. Maybe beautiful."

"Well, I know that, don't I? But what kind of a person
was she?"

"Efficient."

"What's going on here, Pop? I got to go get myself a
pair of pliers, knock you down, and pull a tooth before
you stop gandy-dancing all around?"

"She was tough but fair," he says, like he didn't hear
my last remark.

"She have plenty of that old you-know-what?"

"What the hell's you-know-what?" Mike asks, like
he's a little annoyed.

"Well, they change the name of you-know-what so
much I don't know what to call it anymore," I says.
"Vavoom, it, pizzazz—you know, sex appeal."

"Oh. Well, yeah, she had plenty of you-know-what."

"What's that?"

"Sex appeal."

I'm getting a little suspicious. "Hey, Pop, you ever
have a little you-know-what with Goldie?"

"What's going on here, Jim? You lost your mind? I

break my back getting you a high school education and you can't even speak the language. What's you-know-what supposed to mean this time?"

"You know, a little of the old slap and tickle, a little of the old—"

"Jesus Christ," Mike says, which tells me he's getting really hot under the collar, "what're you talking about? I was married to your mother—God rest her soul. I loved your mother."

"I didn't mean while Ma was alive. I meant maybe before. Maybe after."

"Before, Goldie and me was kids in high school. After, she was working for Carrigan and there was no chance even if either one of us had it in mind," he says, very reasonable, very cool, calm and collected. Which tells me—knowing him the way I do—that he's telling me some but not all. He ain't exactly lying to me but he's sure telling me an Irishman's truth, which is sort of like telling somebody what they'd like to hear—you shouldn't hurt their feelings or get them thinking about things which could bother them but which ain't any of their business.

"You hinting that Ray Carrigan and Goldie was more than employer and employee?"

"Well, first off, they was more like partners," my old man says.

"Also, in the first place, Ray Carrigan was married and still is," I says. "Although it's true that you'll hardly ever see Kate Carrigan from one election year fund-raiser to the next."

"Oh, Carrigan's been married forever all right," Mike says, "but that don't say that old Ray—unlike yours truly—has always practiced self-denial when it comes to the ladies."

"You saying that Johnny McAfee's not exaggerating

when he says that Carrigan's got all them offices so he can write off all them secretaries?"

"Well, I'd hardly take as gospel anything that Johnny McAfee says. I wouldn't hang a man on Johnny McAfee's evidence," Mike says, turning it around on me.

"Well, I didn't say that what McAfee says is true. I'm asking. What I'm doing is asking because if anybody should know is Johnny McAfee lying you should know."

"Why should I know?"

"You been around them both long enough to know."

"So I'd say Johnny McAfee ain't exactly lying but he could be bending the truth a little bit. But you'd have to dig deep to find a trace of scandal against Carrigan."

"That could be just because he's so good at concealing evidence," I says.

Mike gives me a little sideways look but he don't say nothing in exact rebuttal. All he says is, "If I had any secrets I'd tell you, but I don't know. Carrigan likes the ladies now and liked them then. Everybody knows that. That's just it, he likes to play around. You couldn't just play around with Goldie Hanrahan, I don't think. I don't know why you're making innuendos, Jim. It ain't like you."

He gives me a look like he's disappointed in how I turned out to be a gossip after he tried so hard to raise me right, which is this thing he does, turning the tables on me.

"You're the one just brought up the possibility," I says.

"Well, you wanted to know and I'm trying to be cooperative, explore the possibilities with you. Stranger things than a secretary falling in love with her boss have happened and Goldie never got married."

"That's true. So you'd expect—if she had plenty of you-know-what—that she wouldn't go her whole life without a little of you-know-what. Meaning no disrespect," I says.

"Back to talking gobbledygook, are we?" Mike says, picking up the pace as we turn the corner on the way back home like he's in a hurry to tuck into the turkey dinner.

Which is a great dinner.

Even though Mike and me almost get into it again.

It starts when Janet Canarias asks me if it's true that Carrigan asked me to look into Goldie Hanrahan's death.

"Where'd you hear that?" Mike asks.

"I've got friends, Mike," Janet says, giving him her white smile, "just like you've got friends."

"Well, yes," I says, "Mr. Carrigan asked me to have a look around."

"What does that mean exactly?" Janet asks.

"It means have a look around," Mike says.

"I can talk for myself, Pop," I says. "What do you mean what does it mean, Janet?"

"This going to be the dinner table conversation on Thanksgiving Day?" Mike asks.

"I mean, does Carrigan expect you to conceal evidence if you stumble on to something?"

"What would the chairman of the Democratic Party have to hide about a woman who was his right arm for thirty years?" Mike asks.

"What do you mean 'stumble'?" I says at the same time.

"Pass the stuffing, please?" Charlotte says.

While Mike's occupied doing that, I says, "I know there's no love lost between you and Mr. Carrigan, Janet, but I think all he wants is that Goldie Hanrahan's death—in case it could just possibly not be an accident—don't fall through the cracks. Also, if anything turns up, I ain't going to conceal nothing no matter where it points the finger."

"I know that, Jimmy," Janet says, "but does Carrigan know that?"

Just then the phone rings.

Nobody else looks like they can move from the table, so I'm elected. It's for me anyway. Hackman, the medical examiner, is on the other end.

"Catch you at dinner?" he asks.

"How come you ain't at yours?" I asks back.

"I got them piled up down here," he says. "I thought I'd catch up a little when nobody's down here but standby crew and it's nice and quiet."

"Even so you should be home with your family."

"I haven't got a family, Flannery."

"You mean you're all alone on Thanksgiving?"

"Don't get all teary on me, Flannery. I'm doing all right and I've been doing all right for fifteen years."

"I never knew you was alone."

"Forget it. I did the workup on Goldie Hanrahan last night."

"I hope you ain't going to tell me anything in too much detail right after I had my dinner."

"Nothing to tell. The blow to the face killed her. Drove the nose bone into her brain. She wasn't sexually assaulted or molested. Any bruises, scrapes, or concussions are consistent with being knocked off a horse."

"What about her bridgework?"

I'm hoping he ain't going to tell me she swallowed it, though thinking back on it that would've definitely ended everything right there.

"Not in the stomach. Not lodged in the throat or lungs."

"What kind of bridge was it?"

"Removable containing six back teeth, three on each side, and two in the middle."

"So what do you think?"

"I think her horse ran away with her and she got knocked off by a tree limb. Hit her in the mouth and jarred loose her bridgework."

"I had a good look around. I expect the cops have had another look by now, too, though I can't be sure about that. You'd think somebody'd spot a thing like a bridge that big."

"Could've traveled a hell of a distance. Could've landed in the crotch of a tree. Could've got carried off by a squirrel or something. Or how about these kids who found her body? They might've found the bridge and pocketed it, thinking they could hock it for the gold later on."

"Steal from a body and then call the cops?" I says, letting it show how doubtful I am about that.

"Well, maybe the redheaded kid found it after his buddy went to get the police. It's the sort of thing I think that buster might do."

"It's a thought," I says.

"Anyway it's down as death by misadventure."

"And I can tell Ray Carrigan that's that?"

"I already told him."

"Well, thanks," I says. "Hey, before you hang up, you want me to bring you down a nice turkey sandwich?"

"That's really thoughtful of you, Flannery," Hackman says, and I think I detect a little catch in his voice, "but you stay there with your family and friends and I'll stay down here with mine."

He hangs up before I can say anything else.

I go back to the table.

"Another piece of pie before we start clearing the table?" Mary asks.

"Mike an' me'll clear," I says.

"No, no, no," Aunt Sada, Charlotte, Janet, and Mary say all at the same time.

"I'm all for sharing out the burdens of housekeeping," Charlotte says, "but this is Thanksgiving Day and I don't think it'll do any harm to fall back on the old traditions just this once."

The women all pile up the plates and leave me, Mike, and Willy Dink sitting at the table.

"Who was that?" Mike says.

"Hackman. He's got nobody to have Thanksgiving dinner with."

"I didn't know that."

"Me neither. I'll invite him over next year. Anyway, he's working at the morgue today."

"I'd sooner not hear about it," Willy Dink says.

"Nothing to hear about," I says. "Hackman's calling Goldie Hanrahan's death an accident."

Mike nods and sighs like he feels that he can finally say good-bye to an old friend and grieve her passing. "So I guess you can forget about any more investigating," he says.

I give him a nod.

"Willy Dink," I says, "I got to ask you your expert advice."

"About what?"

"Pregnant dogs."

• 9 •

I DON'T KNOW about you, but I can't seem to get anything done over the holidays. From the day before Thanksgiving until the day after New Year I run around like a chicken with my head cut off but by the end of the day I ain't got much done. People are out Christmas shopping, doing this or that. Anyway, they're hard to catch up with and when you do they don't want to be bothered talking to you unless it's something very important or something from which they can make a sizable buck.

Hackman says death by misadventure and everything points to death by misadventure, but something bothers me about the whole business, an easygoing horse, an experienced rider, a wee-hours-of-the-morning ride along a trail seldom ridden. Who knows what people—and horses—'ll do? It could've happened the way it looks. The easy way. The explainable way. More important, what business have I got nosing around when it might be just as well to let the whole sad business fade away?

Anyway, since all I'm going to be doing is bothering people with questions about a friend or acquaintance who died without being able to enjoy all the carols and mistletoe, lights and colored wrappings, and since I don't want to be asking questions about Goldie Hanrahan's death in the first place—no matter what suspicions're nagging at me—I figure I'll just let it drift for a while and maybe Carrigan'll forget all about it in the Christmas rush and maybe we can bury Goldie Hanrahan and let it go at that.

But this business about Goldie Hanrahan's teeth bothers me. The least I can do is check into the possibility that one of them kids found them and decided they weren't going to be very useful to the owner anymore.

So first thing the next morning I get on the phone to the sheriff's office and ask for Koslow.

"What is your business?" the woman on the switchboard asks me.

"It's about something the sheriff and me've been looking into."

"What is your name?"

"Jimmy—James—Flannery."

"Are you a deputy?"

"No, I'm not, I'm—"

"Are you a police officer from a cooperating agency?"

"If I could talk to Sheriff Koslow for fifteen seconds I could save us all a lot of time, please, miss."

"Ms."

"Huh?"

"Ms. I prefer to be called Ms."

"Well, okay, Ms. I can go along with that. I can understand that."

"There's no reason why women's marital status should be announced when addressed and men's not."

"I couldn't agree more. I'll go that one better. I think

everyone should be addressed by their names, so if you'll tell me yours, I won't fall into any traps and call you dear or honey in a mistaken attempt to create the impression of intimacy," I says, giving her a little of the old la-di-da.

"My name is Cheryl Brogan. Are you an attorney, Mr. Flannery?"

"If I said I was an attorney would that get me Sheriff Koslow on the line any quicker?"

"It would probably make no significant difference, except if you lied and told me you were an attorney when you were not an attorney, it would probably lead me to feel ill-disposed toward you."

I don't know, the way this woman's so solemn, if she's pulling my leg Chicago style.

"Ms. Brogan, I got to tell you—can I call you Cheryl? I mean we been talking here so long I'm starting to get the feeling we know each other a long time and are old acquaintances, if not friends."

"You can call me Cheryl if you like, Mr. Flannery."

"And you call me Jimmy."

"No, I'll call you Mr. Flannery. Are you a politician, Mr. Flannery?"

"You know what feeling I'm getting now, Cheryl?"

"What's that, Mr. Flannery?"

"I got the feeling Sheriff Koslow gives you instructions, should a person by the name of Jimmy Flannery call, you should tip him the high sign and give me the runaround while Sheriff Koslow cops a sneak."

"Cops a sneak?"

"Takes a powder."

"Why would Sheriff Koslow want to do that?"

"Because he wants to maintain his reputation for being an honest man when you tell me the sheriff ain't in because he just walked out the door when he found out I was on the phone."

"My God," Cheryl says, suddenly dropping this stiff attitude she's got along with her fancy way of talking, "how'd you pin the tail on the donkey so quick?"

Now I'm talking to a girl from Chicago.

"Bridgeport?" I asks.

"Back of the Yards," she says. "So how'd you know what Stanislaus'd do about taking your calls?"

"I been around the Party since I was in diapers. My old man was a precinct captain for the Democratic Party and I'm a precinct captain for the Democratic Party."

"So what?" she says.

"What do you mean 'so what'?"

"I mean what's it mean being a precinct captain for a Democratic Party what hasn't got an organization worth a nickel?"

"Ain't you heard, young Daley's going to win."

"If you say so."

"You don't think so?"

"There's Vrdolyak."

"A Democrat turned Republican? This is Chicago. You can't go around changing your politics like you change your shorts. He ain't got a Chinaman's."

"What's that?"

"What's what?"

"A Chinaman's."

"Well, you know, a Chinaman's chance?"

"Is that a racist remark?"

Here I am trying to find out if two kids happened to pick up a dead woman's teeth and I'm in a conversation that starts out with a feminist protest, gets into the race for city hall, and ends up with me being accused of being a racist for using an expression that the girl on the other end of the phone is probably too young to know.

"Can we get back to the point?" I says.

"What's the point?"

"Is Koslow out of the office?"

"Sorry," she says.

"So maybe you can help me. He give you any instructions not to help me?"

"Nothing specific."

"So we're inside the letter of the law, so to speak?"

"Depends."

"Can you tell me where Sheriff Koslow put those two kids he picked up the day before Thanksgiving?"

"He didn't put them nowhere. He listens to their story, gives them ice cream cones and soda pop, and lets them go home."

"Where's home?"

"I could look it up."

"Would you do that, Cheryl?"

"You got any clout over to the Eighteenth? I got an aunt lives over there having trouble with the sanitation department."

"You read minds over the phone?"

"What do you mean?"

"I mean you come to the right man. I'm an inspector in the department of sewers. So you got a problem with sanitation you couldn't ask a favor of a better man."

"Isn't it something the way things connect up?"

"It's the Chicago Two-step," I says, and we both have a laugh.

"Wait a second," she says, "I'll go have a look."

In two minutes she's back. She gives me two addresses in a section of town what was knocked down for urban renewal eight years ago and ain't been built up yet.

"How much you want to bet there's a couple of empty lots back-to-back at them addresses?"

"That don't mean my aunt don't get her favor?"

"I don't owe your aunt a favor. I owe you a favor and you want I should do what I can do for your aunt with the sanitation department, you just tell me how I can reach her and consider it done."

She gives me the aunt's address and phone number and then she says, "You married, Jimmy?"

"And my wife's having a baby," I says.

"Wouldn't you know," she says, "all the good ones get snapped up."

So I hang up and take a drive over to the addresses the kids gave the sheriff. A couple of demolition sites sitting side by side, just like I expected.

• 10 •

WAKES AND FUNERALS are occasions when everybody has a chance to sit around and chew the fat or sit staring at the dear departed in the box with nothing to do but think about what put them there.

I put on my black suit and tie and drive on over to the funeral home with Alfie sitting in the back seat. We pull into the parking lot just as Ray Carrigan pulls up in a big black Caddy driven by his secretary, Marilyn.

Carrigan's in back with his poodle dog, Mistinguette, who spots Alfie and starts making a fuss.

Getting out of the car, Marilyn sticks out a leg in a black stocking, then pauses for a New York minute while she gives Alfie a gander.

Hips O'Meara, a precinct captain from the Fourth, comes running over and gives Carrigan a hand out of the car. Carrigan don't need the help but he takes it like it's coming to him.

"How have you been, Hips?" Carrigan asks.

"Fit," O'Meara says. "Very fit, Ray. And yourself?"

"I'm not climbing mountains anymore."

"Well, that's okay, we've climbed our share."

The two old men go toddling into the funeral home and I walk over to see if I can get Marilyn's mind off Alfie.

"Can I help you?" I asks her. She's trying to keep Mistinguette from jumping over the back of the front seat and out of the car to get at Alfie, who's sitting there looking at her with a smug look on his kisser.

"Is that your dog?" Marilyn asks, like she's asking me am I responsible for original sin.

I don't know how I can deny that a dog sitting in the car I just got out of is mine so I says, "Well . . ."

"Is that a yes or a no? Do you own that dog?"

"Nobody owns Alfie. He's like a guest what drops in one day and decides to stay a year."

"That's the dog I caught doing it to Mistinguette."

"Doing what?"

"You know what."

"I'm a married man and I don't know if I should be talking about you-know-what with a pretty girl with her leg showing in front of a funeral home."

She steps out of the car all the way, pushes Mistinguette back one more time, and closes the door.

"I don't know," she says.

Marilyn's one of those people what make remarks like she thinks you was inside her head while she's thinking the thought that's coming out of her mouth.

"Don't know what?" I asks.

"If I should tell Mr. Carrigan what your mutt did to his bitch."

"Well, first of all," I says, "we only got your word for it that Alfie's the dog you saw doing it to Mistinguette. There's lots of dogs around that look like Alfie."

"I don't think so," she says with her lip going all curly.

"In the second place we don't know if there's going to be any consequences of what I'll even concede might have been a chance encounter between my dog and Mr. Carrigan's bitch. Thirdly, if his bitch was in heat—"

"Season."

"In whatever it takes for a bitch to attract, seduce, and otherwise drive a male dog to distraction—"

"And to *action*," she says, giving it a little special emphasis.

"That, too. Anyway, it seems to me as a point of common law that the owner of said female dog should take the responsibility of any consequences arising from letting her run around unattended."

"But I was taking her for a walk."

"Well, now there's another thing. The question comes up did Mr. Carrigan engage a competent guardian for his precious Mistinguette."

She chews that one over. Then she says, "When I tried to intervene, your beast attacked my leg."

"Alfie don't bite."

"I didn't say that he tried to bite me."

"Oh."

I chew that one over. Finally I says, "There's also the question is it the appropriate time to bring up a case of possible assault on a dog when an old friend is about to be laid to rest."

That gives her an out but she only takes half of it. "I won't say anything now," she says, "but I'll be keeping an eye on Mistinguette."

"How's that?"

"Do they have a rabbit test for dogs?"

"Maybe a hamster test."

"Anyway I'll have her examined and if . . ."

She leaves the threat lying there.

I escort her inside the funeral home, my hand under

her elbow going through the door, showing her what a gentleman I am—and like master like dog—taking the chance that somebody gets the news back to Mary that I was seen holding on to a gorgeous young redhead.

Inside the slumber room assigned to Goldie Hanrahan there's a nice crowd. Not as many silver and gray heads as there'd be for a mayor, but more, maybe, than there'd be for an alderman. I show Marilyn to her seat alongside Carrigan and give him my condolences, since being her boss all those years probably makes him as close to being family as Goldie's got. Then I go to the back of the room where I spot my father standing there looking over the sea of black suits and dresses that reaches down to the pale-gray, brushed-steel casket with rose-colored silk lining and pillow upon which Goldie's head is laying up front.

"If I knew when you was coming to pay your respects I could've picked you up," I whispers.

"I got here early," Mike says.

"Oh?" I says.

"I was just going to pop in, say so long, and pop out again. Then I met this one and that one, people I don't see once a year, once every two, three years."

"Old home week."

"Weddings and funerals," Mike says.

We stand there together, shoulder to shoulder, my old man and me, and I'm thinking about how well I know him. All the stories he's told me. All the stories other people have told me about him. I'm thinking that as good as I think I know him I probably don't know him as good as I think I do. He's got secrets just like everybody else. He's got memories he won't tell another soul, just like every person in the room, including me. I'm thinking about how early he might've come and why he wanted to be alone to say good-bye to Goldie Hanrahan, who, he says, was no more than a friend, maybe only an old acquaintance.

Then, for no reason I can explain, I'm thinking about that old one, the one about the killer returning to see his victim off, and I'm looking around the room at Ray Carrigan, Sidney Hackman, Smith Jarwolski, the police superintendent, Ed Keady, committeeman for the Forty-seventh Ward, Jack Reddy, the Water Department super, Big Ed Lubelski, the warlord of the Thirty-second, Jerry Killian, the alderman from the First, and all the old, gray warlords and war-horses, sitting there saying good-bye to one of their own. A woman who'd been a power in the city. A woman who might've still been a power, finagling this or that, cutting deals, refusing to stay out in the pasture. A woman who'd been catnip to the men when she'd been a girl and even after.

A woman who'd maybe had a secret that somebody wanted kept secret.

Somebody sitting right there in the room.

• 11 •

IT'S GETTING VERY HOT from so many bodies stuffed into the room. The smell of the ocean of flowers is so sweet my stomach's starting to turn.

First this man and then that one gets up and tiptoes up the aisle on the way to the gents' room downstairs. Some would like to get away from the smell just like I'm ready to do. Some want a smoke, and some want a little nip from a hip flask or a bottle.

Mike gives me a dig in the ribs and points to the door with his chin. He's ready for a little relief hisself.

We join the march down the carpeted stairs. The basement's deep enough you know you don't got to keep on whispering and mumbling. The men's voices come rumbling up the stairwell until we get to the rest room on one side of the hallway and the smoking room on the other.

My old man goes one way and I go the other.

In the smoking room you'd think it was a political convention except they ain't counting votes or cutting deals, they're talking about the dear departed.

Wally Dunleavy, Streets and Sanitation, is sitting there with Smith Jarwolski, in full dress uniform, and Hicky Isadore, from the Board of Education.

"Hungry for knowledge, Goldie was," Isadore's saying. "Came to me twenty years ago, tells me she's ashamed she never finished high school. Can she go back to school at her age and get her diploma? I tell her she can take a test that'll give her credits for life experience. She says she's not so sure what she's learned since she quit school in the seventh grade could apply toward a diploma. I told her give it a try."

Dunleavy and Jarwolski are nodding their heads and looking at the toes of their highly polished shoes, agreeing with every word Isadore's saying, having heard this story maybe a hundred times before.

"She sits for the test," Isadore goes on. "She scores a hundred in civics, mathematics, history, and—you wouldn't expect it—general science."

"How's that?" Dunleavy says, pushing the storyteller along.

"She knows everything there is to know about metallurgy. Remarkable."

"She get her diploma?" I asks, because it looks like the story's going to end there.

The three old men, still active, still powerful, but under the shadow of eternity every one, look up at me like I'm a voice from another world.

"She do good at everything else?" I asks.

"Zip in home economics, geography, and English."

"So what?" Jarwolski says, like he's ready to defend Goldie against my attack.

"So I'm just asking. Just sticking a foot in the conversation."

"I know you, Flannery. You stick a foot in a conversation, you're nosing around looking for some dirt."

"That's no way to talk to a city employee," Dunleavy says, sort of leaping to my defense. "Especially a man who works for Sewers, which is under Streets and Sanitation. Especially one who works for my old friend Chips Delvin."

"I know all about Chips Delvin setting this Flannery up in business down in the sewers, making him a precinct captain over to the Twenty-seventh," Jarwolski says.

"That was fifteen years ago. More," Isadore says softly.

"Well, I was against it then and I'm against it now," Jarwolski says.

"You weren't against it," Dunleavy says. "You didn't even know young Flannery back then."

"I knew young Flannery the minute I set eyes on him. You forget I was at the dinner over to Poppsie Hanneman's when this one walks in and practically threatens Carmine DiBella, a loyal Democrat, in front of thirty people."

"Poppsie Hanneman and Goldie Hanrahan was good friends, wasn't they?" Dunleavy says, like he's asking for a point of order.

"Poppsie Hanneman's mother, Jessie, and Goldie was girls together in the Tenth Ward," Jarwolski says.

"Rumor had it at the time that both Jessie and Goldie had an eye on Barney "Knockwurst" Hanneman and his cold-cut fortune," Isadore says. "He was as happy as a pig on ice, beautiful girls playing up to him."

"Ain't it funny how he couldn't make up his mind between two gorgeous Irish girls and ends up marrying the daughter of one of them?" Dunleavy says.

"Nobody ever said old Knockwurst was dumb," Isadore says.

Mike comes into the room and walks over to where I'm standing.

Right off, Jarwolski says to him, "Hey, Michael

Flannery, why don't you teach this kid of yours to mind his own business?''

"What business is that?"

"Moving shit."

"Hey," Dunleavy says sharply, like a barking dog.

"You got a wild hair, Jarwolski?" Mike says.

"I'm just saying your kid's always sticking his nose into police business."

"What's he done lately?"

"He's trying to besmirch the good name of Goldie Hanrahan."

"How do you come by that?"

"Sheriff Koslow informs me."

"You Polacks really like to gossip, don't you?"

"Not as much as you Irish."

My old man and Jarwolski seem to be having a good time nipping at each other so I drift away, thinking about how a lot of people are getting the word that I'm looking into the death of Goldie Hanrahan when actually I ain't doing any such thing and in fact, have pretty much decided, on the evidence, there's nothing much to look into.

"Over here, Jimmy," somebody calls to me.

I look over at this couch where Carrigan and my old Chinaman, Delvin, are sitting side by side.

"I didn't even see you come in," I says to Delvin, going over to shake his hand.

"Get a chair, Jimmy. Drag it over here."

I reach out for a folding chair leaning against the wall, unfold it, and set it up by their knees.

"Ray here tells me you're doing a little job of work for him," Delvin says in his confidential voice.

"Well, actually, I was going to ask for an appointment early next week and talk about that very thing," I says.

"How's that?" Carrigan says.

"I don't see what I can do. You got the call from Hackman?"

"I did."

"Well, then, you know what he found out about Goldie Hanrahan."

"What's that?"

"That she wasn't raped or assaulted. That she probably died by misadventure."

"Is that what you think?"

"It's what Hackman thinks. It's what Sheriff Koslow seems to think. It's what Police Superintendent Jarwolski thinks."

"He complain about you looking into this matter for me?"

"He ain't happy about it."

"No kidding? What business is it of his? It's not his jurisdiction. Why's he trying to put a clamp on it?"

"I didn't say he was trying to put a clamp on it. I just said he made a remark, he don't like it. There's other people don't seem to like it."

Delvin's sitting there listening to the conversation with a bland look on his face like he's hardly interested in what's being said.

"And why is that, do you suppose?" Carrigan says, grinning like the cat what ate the canary and tipping me the wink as he struggles to lift up his hip and dig into his pocket. "You're not afraid of opposition, are you, Flannery?"

"Anybody who's not afraid when important people let him know that what he's doing ain't to their liking is a damn fool," I says. "Besides, it ain't just me I'm concerned about."

"Who else?"

"You, Mr. Carrigan. I keep going on with this, you might have to take a little heat."

"It's nice of you to worry about my health, Jimmy, but I think I can take just about anything that comes my way."

I'm thinking that some people would say that he don't care what trouble he stirs up because a man his age's got nothing to lose, but anybody, especially a politician, no matter what age he happens to be, has got his reputation to lose, his immortality to lose, his legend to lose.

He finally gets what he was digging for. He comes up with a key and hands it to me.

"This here's the key to Goldie Hanrahan's flat. Whatever you're going to say about breaking and entering don't say because I'm giving you permission to look around."

Delvin and me are probably looking at him a certain way because he says, "Don't give me the old one-eye. I'm finally beyond such shenanigans. Goldie worked for me a long time and we was friends for longer than that. She never trusted the cops or the ambulance to get to her on time if she was taken serious during the night so she gave me a key. She knew I'd be there to help inside of five minutes."

"We weren't suggesting, Ray," Delvin says in an oily voice meant to suggest everything and then some.

Carrigan slaps Delvin's knee and cackles like an old hen. "Would that it were so, Chips. Would that it were so." Then he stops laughing, presses my hand with the key in it, and says, "Just find out two things for me, Flannery. What was Goldie doing out there that time of the morning? Where's her teeth? Go find that poor woman's teeth before we have to go ahead and bury her without them."

He struggles up and out of the leather sofa.

"Just bring anything you find to me first. Remember we're in this thing together." He stands there, tottering a little on his old legs. "Looks like young Daley's going to win this one."

"But will it ever be the same, Ray?" Delvin says.

"You mean will the machine start running the way it used to? No, it won't. These are different times. There's not much patronage to give out anymore. The courts took care of that. But there'll still be opportunities to be had. Being the warlord of a ward might mean a little something once again."

He toddles away, leaving me and my old Chinaman to chew that one over.

"He's not suggesting that Jarwolski knows there's a crime here and wants it covered up?" I says.

"Who knows what he thinks? Do the job he asks you to do. Go through the motions. Keep the old man happy."

"That don't seem to be a very good reason to play elaborate games," I says.

He raises his eyebrows like he's startled and astounded to hear me complain about playing games, which he probably thinks I'm playing all the time.

"Well, do it because your dog did it to his dog and you'd do well to have Carrigan owing you a big favor."

"How'd you know about Alfie and his dog?" I asks.

"Ah, Jesus, Jimmy, this old fox ain't deaf, dumb, and blind yet."

• 12 •

FINDING A FRIEND'S MURDERER is one thing. Helping out an influential person like Carrigan is another thing. But nosing around in a person's private life when they probably died by accident is going too far.

So here I am with the key to Goldie's flat in my hand and feeling bad about it.

I'm also excited and curious about what I might find inside the legendary Goldie Hanrahan's apartment.

The key slides in, then catches. For a minute there I got to jiggle it, work it in and out a hair until I can turn it. That could mean the lock's a little worn or it could be somebody's jimmied the door and damaged the pins.

The door swings open and I step inside into a little hall. What they call a foyer. It's got striped cream-and-green wallpaper. There's a wide doorway into a living room and a short passage off to the right with a gilt mirror at the end of it. Also a doorway that probably leads to the back of the apartment, the kitchen and the service porch. Maybe a maid's room, which in these

grand old apartments most people use for an extra bedroom or a place for storage.

The other way goes to a little powder room. I step
inside and take a look. Just a toilet and a sink. Old-
fashioned wallpaper in a pattern of small roses. Guest
towels hung over a brass bar. A big clamshell filled with
little pieces of soap in different colors and shapes. Fussy
and fancy.

The foyer's gloomy and the living room ain't much
better because the windows are covered in heavy gray
velvet drapes. I don't know if Goldie left them that way
when she went out the morning she got killed or if
somebody—the cleaning lady, somebody—has been in
since and closed them; the sun shouldn't fade the carpet
when it comes pouring in late in the afternoon.

I go over and look for the pull to open them up.
There's a little motor does the job at the touch of a
button. The drapes glide back and the morning light
comes in through the windows but it don't do much
good since winter's finally socked in and the cloud cover
over Chicago's so thick you can't see even a wink of
sun. I punch the button and the drapes glide shut.

The drapes is gray and the furniture is rose and green.
All velvet, too. There's little tables like you see in English television historical programs all over the place,
convenient to the sofas and easy chairs in case you got
guests in for tea.

There's some prints, still lifes with lots of flowers and
vegetables, and old-fashioned people in front of thatched
cottages or by the seaside, in gold frames. Plus a portrait
of Goldie which looks to me like it was done by one of
them artists who paints your picture from a photograph.

She's wearing a green satin evening gown off the shoulders and her hair's piled up on top of her head like she
was going out for the evening.

At first I think it looks like her, then I realize it looks like her when she was laying in the coffin, only younger, but not like she did when she was alive.

I wander through the dining room into the kitchen. All nicely furnished, appliances the top of the line, ruffled curtains at the window over the sink. Yellow and blue.

There's not a crumb around the toaster, the oven's clean as a whistle, the glasses in the cabinets sparkling. There's a glass, a coffee mug, a small plate, a knife, and a spoon in the dish rack.

I open up the dishwasher. Nothing in it.

The bedroom's more of the same. Neat and clean. Clothes—nice dresses, some cocktail and evening gowns, even furs—lined up in long rows in the walk-in closet. Shoes and slippers lined up on shelves.

I open the drawers in the tallboy and the chest. Her sweaters and underwear are separated into neat piles. I don't go poking through her stuff. I lift the edges of each folded garment though and check to see if she's got a diary or something like that hidden away. There's nothing.

Her dresser's practically covered with fancy cut-glass perfume bottles and pictures in small silver frames of Goldie with different people. Most of the men are in tuxedos and Goldie's always in a gown. I recognize four mayors, Daley, Bilandic, Byrne, and Washington. There's a couple of United States senators and even a picture of Goldie with ex-presidents Johnson, Reagan, and Carter.

Also half the power brokers in the city, going back to Hizzoner's reign, are represented.

And Carmine DiBella, the Mafia don, Dunleavy, the head of Streets and Sanitation, Ed Keady, Jerry Killian, and Big Ed Lubelski, leaders of the Forty-seventh, First, and Thirty-second wards, Jack Reddy, now the supervisor of the water department, and plenty of others I know and some I don't.

I go back to where the maid's room was when even middle class people had maids. I try the knob but the door's locked. I got this kid, lives next door to Mary and me, taught me how to pick locks. What kids know nowadays can make you wonder. It takes me maybe a minute, maybe a minute and a half, to jimmy the door and step inside.

She's been using it for a bedroom just like I figured except there's an air about this room which gives me the feeling it's the only one that's really been lived in.

It's a plain room with a single bed that looks like it was slept in, a small overstuffed chair with a chintz slipcover and a shawl tossed over the back of it, a dresser with a mirror, and a little pine wardrobe since there's no closet.

The wardrobe's got two or three cotton house dresses in it, a ratty pair of slippers, and a chenille bathrobe with most of the pom-poms worn off the sleeves and back. It could be the maid's things, but somehow I know they ain't the maid's things.

There's a rollaway table with a nineteen-inch television on it.

There's some framed pictures on the walls. What I guess is her mother and father on their wedding day. And some of them stiff-posed pictures which an old-time photographer retouched and colored until the people—which I figure is her grandparents—look dead.

There's more photos in frames on the dresser, but the frames are imitation tortoiseshell or plain wood.

Goldie's in these pictures, too, except she's always with just one other person, a different man in each one, and the clock's turned back forty years.

There's not a woman in any of them, not even in the background.

I recognize Ray Carrigan from back then. He looks

like Spencer Tracy. There's Smith Jarwolski when he was a patrolman in uniform, and my old Chinaman, Delvin, when he was a much younger man. I think I recognize Vito Velletri, the warlord of the Twenty-fifth.

There's one more picture. A picture of Goldie with my old man. It must be 1951, '52, because he's in uniform. The Korean War was on, he was about twenty-six years old, and he was just about ready to marry my mother. They're at some kind of amusement park. There's a sign in the background. I get my nose up close and I can just barely make out the word *City* and the letters *tic* in front of it. Atlantic City?

All of the pictures seem to be from back around then. Say the early fifties into the sixties.

Goldie looks like she's in her late teens or early twenties. A very beautiful girl who smiles these tight little smiles—she had bad teeth even back then—but even in such small pictures you can see she's got something special on the ball.

I wonder about all the places the snapshots could've been taken. I wonder who took them. It could be they was all taken by different photographers like the ones that hang around amusement piers. I wonder if these are photos of Goldie on her day off having a date with a different boyfriend.

Except for the one with my father taken in Atlantic City. They'd have had to travel to get there on the East Coast.

There's one more snapshot of Goldie. She's holding a baby in her arms. There's no man in the picture. I wonder which one of the men in the other pictures took the snap.

I take the photos of my old man, Ray Carrigan, and Chips Delvin and put them in my pocket, knowing that somewhere down the road I could be charged with breaking and entering, interfering with a police investigation, suppressing evidence, burglary, and petty theft.

There's a telephone on the floor by the bed and a little book alongside it.

I sit down on the bed and pick up the book. It's an appointment calendar. I look at the last day when Goldie was alive. There's four entries. I hear a key in the front door. I go out through the kitchen and the back door to the service landing, closing it with a lot of care.

Then I stand there wondering what I should do. Finally I bend down on one knee and look through the old fashioned keyhole.

I see a Latino woman about fifty come into the kitchen. She stands in the middle of the floor, like she's listening. She shakes her head, a sad look on her face. Then she takes off her coat. She's wearing a blue smock. It's the maid.

I take the service elevator down to the basement and walk over to the park where I can sit on a bench and read.

• 13 •

I LOOK THROUGH the appointment book. It's nothing special. It looks like every appointment book I ever seen except maybe it's a little neater than most, since Goldie was a secretary and Carrigan's executive assistant all those years.

The page on the day of her death has five notations.

The first note says, "Shedd, B.B.?" The next one says, "Sissy—Breakfast." The next one is "John M.—Lunch." "R.C." is the next, and the last one says "D.D.S.—3:00."

I sit there working out what I can from not very much.

When you shorthand somebody's name with initials it probably means you know them pretty good or their names is fresh in your memory.

So it figures, until I find out otherwise, that R.C. stands for Ray Carrigan.

Because she uses the whole first name you got to figure she's got lots of last names in her address book start with *M* but only one John M.

She uses the whole last name, Shedd, which tells me it's somebody she's just met so that she's afraid she could forget it and initials won't be enough to remind her who it is.

Sissy I don't know if it's a good friend, not a good friend, or she just wrote it down like that for no particular reason. We don't always do the same things the same way.

D.D.S. stymies me for a minute. Why would she use three initials? Then I flash on her nickname and her missing bridgework and I'm willing to bet D.D.S. stands for doctor of dental science.

That's as far as I can get sitting on the bench, so I go back to her apartment house and take the elevator back up to her floor and walk along the corridor until I come to her door and knock on it.

After about a minute I knock again.

A voice from the other side says, "Wha' do you wan'?"

There's a lot of city employees besides cops and firemen what carry badges. I got a little badge pinned inside my wallet because sometimes you got trouble with a backed-up sewer line into a house and you got to get in there to have a look so you got to show something official so people will let you in.

So I take out my wallet and hold the badge up to the spy hole for a couple seconds and then close it up and put it back in my pocket hoping she'll think I'm a cop without me having to lie out loud.

There's another little delay while she thinks it over and then she opens the door but leaves it on the chain.

"Wha' you wan'?" she says again.

She's got a nice coffee-colored face, sweet and calm, except her eyes are rimmed with red because she's been crying.

"I come about Ms. Hanrahan."

"She had an accident. She's dead," she says, and her face twists up in a little spasm like she's going to let go again but she gets hold of herself.

"I know. That's what I come about."

"Yes?" she says, but she don't open the door.

"You happen to know the name of her dentist?"

A little frown puckers up the skin between her eyes like she's wondering what I want to know that for.

"I don't like to upset you with such things, ma'am," I says, "but Ms. Hanrahan's teeth was damaged and the undertaker'd like to see her X rays so he can . . . reconstruct the face."

She winces again. "She's already laid out. I wen' to see her," she says.

"So you could tell she don't look natural."

She takes the door off the chain and opens up.

"Please, come in," she says. "I go fin' Ms. Hanrahan's book."

"I take it you're Ms. Hanrahan's housekeeper?" I says.

"I'm jus' the cleaning lady. I come in half a day, t'ree times a week."

"Well, that's being a housekeeper," I says, smiling at her.

"I suppose so. You wan' to wait in the living room? I t'ink it'll be all righ'."

I follow her into the room I was just in fifteen minutes before.

"What can I call you, miss?" I asks.

"Connie. Ms. Hanrahan always called me Connie," she says, and hurries out of the room, her hand getting a handkerchief out of the pocket of her smock.

She's opened the gray velvet drapes. The overcast is breaking up and there's a slice of sun on the carpet. Even so I get the feeling again that the flat was hardly lived in, like Goldie had earned the fancy coveted flat in the expensive building but never really felt comfortable in it.

I stand up when Connie comes back with the address book. The courtesy flusters her a little so she don't hesitate handing it over.

"It's cold out today, ain' it?" she says.

"It surely is," I says.

"Maybe you'd like a cup of coffee?"

"Only if you'll have one with me."

She blushes and says, "You t'ink tha' would be all righ'?"

"I don't think Ms. Hanrahan would mind we had a cup of coffee together."

"No, she wouldn'. Plenty times she ask me to sit down have a cup of coffee wit' her. Talked to me about when she was a young woman jus' makin' her way out of the tenemen's."

"I'd like to hear some of that," I says, like now I'm an old friend of Goldie's and not just the cop I'm sort of pretending to be.

"I make the coffee," she says, and leaves the room.

I sit down and go through the book. First I look up Shedd, but I can't find any Shedd in it.

Then I check out John M's and come up with three. John Markowitz, John MacNamara, and John Milholland. I write down their addresses and phone numbers on one of the three-by-five cards I carry around with me when I'm looking into something.

I find the dentist listed. Dr. Harry Slaughter. I can imagine the jokes the poor guy must get about that. I take down the vitals.

Just to be on the safe side I go through the C's and find out that Ray Carrigan ain't the only R.C. in it. There's also a Robert Campo, so I write that down, too.

Connie comes in with the coffee in two mugs on a

plastic tray with some pink packets of sweetener and a small container of low-fat milk and sets it down on the table.

"Ms. Hanrahan don' keep no sugar or cream in the house."

"That's all right. I take mine black half the time anyway."

She sits down and waits for me to pick up my mug before she picks up hers. Neither of us puts anything in it and we both take sips at the same time to test how hot it is. Just then a wind comes blasting in off the lake and rattles the windows. We both look over there like we think somebody's trying to get in, then we look at each other and grin and take another swallow of the hot coffee.

"You fin' the dentist's name?" she asks.

"I think so. This the only address book she keeps?"

"I don' know," she says, frowning like my question puzzles her.

"I mean like she could have a personal address book and a business address book."

"Maybe she got one over to her office."

"She's got an office? I didn't know she had an office. What would she want an office for? She's retired over five years."

Connie shrugs her shoulders as though she don't know and she don't care.

"Maybe she's got business. Importan' people like Ms. Hanrahan always got business."

And important people like Goldie Hanrahan what retire from government service got plenty of inside dope, clout, and savvy to sell. So they set up as consultants and make five times as much for introducing this person to that person than when they was one of the persons other persons wanted to be introduced to.

I wondered if Goldie'd set herself up in the influence and favor business and thought it smarter not to work out of her home.

"You know where this office is?"

"No, but she give me the number in case I ever had to get her and she wasn' here at home."

"You happen to know it off hand?" I asks with my pen ready to write it down on one of my cards.

She rattles it off no trouble like it was a number she was used to.

"You call her at the office a lot?" I asks.

"Wha' you mean?"

"I mean either you called her a lot or you got a good memory for numbers. I got a very bad memory for numbers. Sometimes I have a hard time remembering my own."

"Oh, me, too. I mean, how often you call yourself?"

"So you called Ms. Hanrahan at the office a lot?"

"Only lately. For the las' couple of weeks. Excep' for las' week. She wanted me to call her three times a day and tell her was everyt'ing all right aroun' here."

"What'd she mean by that?"

"I don' know. She jus' told me anythin' out of the ord'nary—that's wha' she said, 'out of the ord'nary' —happens, like a telephone call the party wouldn' leave a name or somebody knockin' on the door to deliver somethin' she don' order or somebody hangin' aroun' outside watchin' the windows, I should call her righ' up an' tell her abou' it."

"What about last week?"

"She tol' me not to worry abou' it no more."

"Ms. Hanrahan a nice person to work for?"

Tears come spilling out of Connie's eyes again. She sops them up with her handkerchief.

"The bes'," she says. "Sometimes, like when we was

cleanin' up for spring, you know, she'd put on an ol' dress and tie her hair in a towel and clean along wit' me. She never treated me like I was nothin' but a person wha' cleaned her house. It was like we was friends.''

"How long you work for her?"

"T'ree years come Christmas."

I'm trying to figure out a way to ask about the locked room without giving it away that I been in the flat already.

"So you started working for her at Christmastime?"

Connie nods her head and takes another sip of coffee, holding the mug in both hands like it's giving her comfort.

"I always get a little sad around Christmastime," I says.

"Me, too," she says.

"Reminds me of how good it was when I was a kid and how, no matter how good it is now, it never seems as good as it did when you was a kid."

"Tha's righ'," she agrees.

"You remember anything special about when you was a kid at Christmastime?"

"I remember the smell of cookin' in the house. I remember the piñatas."

"I wonder did Ms. Hanrahan remember anything special like that."

Connie starts to say something but then she thinks better of it and just says, "I suppose."

I give a little laugh like I know I'm about to be nosy but I can't help it. "You know, while you was making the coffee I needed to use the facility and I went out in the hallway and tried a door and it was locked. That a closet?"

Connie smiles a little, like me saying what I said right out the way I done convinces her I'm okay. "Oh, no, tha' used to be the maid's room."

"So now it's just a junk room, that it? I could sure use a junk room where me and my wife live but the flat's too small so I got to shove everything downstairs in the bin in the cellar or fill up the hall closet."

"No, Ms. Hanrahan don' use it for a junk room."

"Oh? What does she use it for?"

"I t'ink she used it for like a shrine, a place where she could remember and like that."

"Shrine to what?"

Connie gives one of those patented Latin shrugs that says ten times as much as words could say. "Who knows? To when she was young, maybe."

I get up and Connie sees me to the door.

"By the way," I says, "you happen to know if Ms. Hanrahan had a friend she called Sissy?"

"Tha' be Mrs. Palou. Shirley Palou. She lives in a building two doors down the block, the other side of the street."

• 14 •

THE MINUTE SHE OPENS THE DOOR I recognize Sissy Palou from the funeral parlor. She was a little woman with bleached hair and silver fox furs around her shoulders sitting in the first row near the head of the coffin crying into a couple of handkerchiefs, one in each hand.

Now she's wearing a negligee, with a big collar of marabou feathers, which she fills out like toothpaste in a tube. She looks squeezable and you don't have to have the sharpest eyes in the world to see that she was a knockout once upon a time.

She reminds me a little bit of this ex-madam what lived in the same apartment house where this photographer killed the girlfriend of a friend of mine, and I wonder if Ms. Palou wasn't in the same trade.

Like she's reading my mind, Sissy says, "Yes, I was."

"Was what?" I says, like somebody what just fell off the turnip truck.

"I was a lady of the evening, a party girl, a companion

of elderly gentlemen, and the lover of many a young one who sometimes was a gentleman and sometimes was not."

Her eyes're sad, but her lipsticked mouth is grinning, showing off the dimples at the corners of her lips.

"I saw you at Goldie's lying in," she goes on. "Your hair caught my eye. I've always been partial to redheads."

"And I've always been partial to platinum blondes."

"Well, ain't you sweet," she says, grabbing me by the sleeve and pulling me inside. "Don't worry. I ain't going to jump on you. I just need a friend to talk to. I need a friend who was a friend of Goldie's."

I let myself be dragged inside, through the hall and into the parlor—which is all pink, gold, and white like her—but I tell her I'm not really a friend of Goldie's though I'd be happy to listen to what she's got to tell me.

"Sure," she says after she's got me on the couch and sits herself down beside me, "you'll listen. Ain't that why you just come knocking at my door? I know you and I know what you do."

"Oh?" I says.

"You're an undercover cop," she says.

"What?" I almost yells, truly startled that anybody should say such a thing about me. "Whatever give you that idea?"

"You can't kid me. I know you're supposed to have a job inspecting the sewers, working for old Chips Delvin. Also that you're a precinct captain for the old Democratic machine, which ain't doing so good lately."

"We got Hizzoner's kid, young Richard, running this time," I says.

"Even if he wins, the old days is gone. But don't try getting me off the point. I'm saying all that business you do in the sewers and the ward's just smoke and whistles. Who you working for? Smith Jarwolski? Wally Dunleavy? Some secret commission?"

I got the notion that I'll get more out of her if I go along than if I don't, so I sort of cock an eyebrow and smile this smile like I seen Cary Grant smile in several of his pictures where he was saying no but smiling yes, if you know what I mean.

"I don't hear you denying it," she says.

"Well, I denied it once," I says, "and I'm not the kind of person likes to chew his cabbage twice."

"It figures. You went up against Carmine DiBella at Poppsie Hanneman's house a few years ago. You went against the party when you fingered Big Buck Bailey and Pat Connell for that killing in the steam room with the gorilla. You brought down Cheech and Little Foot with the alligators. You nailed that crazy photographer what was thinning out the turkey herd."

"How do you know all this?" I says.

She puts a red fingernail up to her lower eyelid and pulls it down. "I got my sources," she says.

"Well, some of it was in the papers and on the news, but how do you know about I had an exchange of views with Mr. DiBella over to Poppsie Hanneman's?"

"Poppsie's a friend of mine. I know her since she was a kid."

"I used to spend some time with Poppsie," I says.

"Don't I know that? Girls talk. Hold it. I know what you're thinking. Poppsie never worked for me. Never worked for nobody as far as I know—and I'd know. She only worked for herself. We ain't the same generation either but that don't keep us from being friends. Her and me and Jessie and Goldie, we all come from the Tenth. Our fathers, brothers, and husbands—if any—all worked in the steel mills. We spoke the same language. We was friends."

"Poppsie and Goldie?"

"I don't know about that. I meant I was friends with Jessie and Poppsie, and I was friends with Goldie."

She runs down like an old clock, the memories of youth getting clogged in her throat, bringing fresh tears to her eyes.

"So can I get you a refreshment?" she asks.

"Nothing, thanks."

"Well, you don't mind, I'll have myself a little toddy. I usually don't drink during daylight hours but I'm feeling blue and a little sip'll ease the hurt."

She goes to a little mirrored bar and pours herself a double shot from a decanter with a top that plays "How Dry I Am," adds two ice cubes from a little undercounter fridge and a splash of water, then comes back to sit down beside me again.

"Had my first drink in the company of Goldie Hanrahan. We was fifteen, sixteen. It wasn't whiskey, though, it was champagne. Some cheap bottle. Come to think of it, it was probably nothing but white wine with some fizz shot in it. What could we afford, a couple of brats working in the five-and-dime?"

"What was the occasion?" I asks.

She cocks an eye at me as though wondering if she should let me in on this news which is almost forty years old.

"Was it a celebration?" I asks.

She gives a little laugh, midway between a snort and a giggle. "Celebration? Come to think of it you might call it that. I suppose we might've even said so at the time, but if we said so it was with a curly lip."

I wait for her to go on. Her eyes go dreamy and her face gets young while she brings it all back to mind.

"I don't know what we thought we was doing. Goldie'd found out she was going to have a baby."

It got quiet in the room. I could hear a clock somewhere ticking time away. I felt like I was caught in a bubble.

Then Sissy took a breath and broke the spell.

"No, I don't think it was exactly a celebration," she says. "More like a wake for our girlhood. I'd already had three scares and an abortion." She looks at me very sharp. "You making judgments?"

"I got enough trouble wiping my own nose," I says. "I got my ideas. I got my beliefs. But I don't go around stuffing them in other people's pockets and I don't go around making remarks about what other people're carrying in theirs."

"Well, okay," she says, like I'd just barely missed insulting her that time.

"Goldie have an abortion?" I asks, afraid that maybe she'll think that I'm getting too nosy and cut me off.

But either she don't think the question's out of line or she figures the company's worth it because she shakes her head and says, "Abortions weren't all that easy to come by. I nearly died from the one I had done and Goldie knew it. Also, she was still tied to the church more than somewhat. Did novenas and made her confession every week. She did a novena and prayed for a natural miscarriage. I told her that praying for it and doing something about it didn't seem all that different to me, but she said it was a lot different. If God wanted her to have the baby she'd have it, husband or no husband. I asked her was she going to get the beast for the burden."

I guess I'm just staring at her like I'm stupid or something because she goes on and tells me that she meant get the guy what got her in a family way. I was afraid to ask her who the man might be. As it turns out she would've told me if she'd known, I think, because she pulls a little face and says, "We was best friends but she'd never cop on that one even though I asked her a hundred times."

"Well, you must've known who her boyfriend was."

"Boy*friends*," Sissy says, hitting the last part of it hard. "Boy*friends*. Goldie wasn't just a beautiful kid. She had something else going for her. I wasn't so hard on the eyes myself, but if Goldie and me met a couple of guys along the avenue or in the park, they'd both be after her and she'd have to make her pick before the one she didn't fancy'd give me a tumble. It used to burn me up sometimes, you can bet."

"You know her boyfriends?"

"Most of them. Wait. Let's say I thought I did. Some things Goldie could be very quiet about. Very secret. Very sly. Like who was the father of her kid for instance."

"Could you name me some of the ones you knew about?"

"I suppose you only want the special ones?"

"Since I don't know how it could help, I suppose it don't matter. On the other hand, if her getting killed out in the woods has anything to do with her having a baby almost forty years ago, it's more likely it'd be connected with somebody she had something special going with than some guy she picked up in the park or on the street."

"Or it could be one of the somebodys she never told me about."

"Well, how about you tell me the names of the men you remember having anything friendly to do with Goldie."

She starts naming names. There's more than a handful. She names Velletri and Carrigan and Delvin and others, some of which I know and some of which I don't.

She names my old man and she don't name Jarwolski and she don't name a couple of others who were known as hounds for the ladies and who was also in the political crowd Goldie seemed to've run around with.

So now comes the big question. "Where's the kid now?" I asks.

She shrugs her shoulders and the feather collar waves in the breeze all around her cheeks and chin.

"No idea?" I asks.

"Not a clue."

"She give it out for adoption?"

"She tried to keep it. She raised it until it was about five. Then she was offered opportunities that made it harder and harder for her to have a career and be a mother."

She says this with a little edge of bitterness and disdain in her voice, like if she'd had a kid she'd've been able to do both, make a good living and raise the kid.

"Gave it to a relative to raise," she says.

"What relative?"

"Maybe her mother. Or maybe her sister. She had a sister living here in Chicago, had kids of her own, so maybe she left the kid with her sister."

"You remember the sister's name?"

"Mabel. I think it was Mabel."

"You happen to remember Mabel's last name?"

"Stukey. Pickle. Something like that. It's been a while."

"That's okay," I says, "I'll get it off Goldie's insurance records. Maybe she made her kid or her sister her beneficiary."

"You got to understand she wouldn't've been abandoning it. She'd be doing what she thought was best. She got her foot on the ladder. Got herself a job as secretary to Ray Carrigan and there was no way them days she could've held down a job like that and looked for promotions with a kid to take care of. Goldie was ambitious.''

"Was the baby a boy or a girl?"

"A boy. Didn't I say that?"

"You remember him?"

"Didn't see much of him. Goldie and me had a spat, you understand?"

"About what?"

"About her not sharing her connections with me."

"You mean you wanted a secretary's job, too?"

She laughs like I meant to be funny and she enjoys the joke.

"Oh, no, I didn't want no eight to six. I just wanted the connections. I mean she had a lot of boyfriends before and after she had the kid. I figured she wouldn't be seeing so much of them anymore. I figured they could be looking for a little comfort. I was just setting up in business, you understand, and a nice address book's the best thing a young entrepreneur, just starting out, can have. Ain't that right?"

"So when was the last time you talked to Goldie Hanrahan?" I asks.

She stares at me again, her eyes filling up. "Oh, hell, I don't remember the exact date."

"But you knew about her giving up the kid five years later."

"Well, I asked around about her, you know? I still liked her a lot even after we had the fight. I wanted to make it up but I was too stubborn and she was too stubborn.

"Don't ask me why, after nearly forty years, I suddenly got the nerve to call her up. But anyway I did. Last Sunday I got to feeling really blue so I called her up and she was so happy to hear from me. She told me she thought maybe I was long dead and gone and I said I knew she wasn't because she showed up in the newspapers all the time going to this fancy party or some convention. We started crying so hard it's a wonder it didn't spill into the telephones and short out the system."

"So you made a date to meet?" I says.

"That's right."

"For breakfast Wednesday morning?"

"I waited for her for over an hour but she never showed up," Sissy says in a voice so soft I could hardly hear it.

The tears spill over and run down her cheeks, cutting little glassy rivers in her powdered cheeks.

"I shoulda swallowed my pride and called her years ago," she says. "You know the funniest thing of all?"

"What's that?"

"When we found out where we was living we couldn't believe it. For the last four, five years, we been living only two blocks away from each other. For the last year we been living right across the street. We never bumped into one another on the street. How do you figure a crazy thing like that?"

· 15 ·

JUST MARY AND ME are sitting down to supper. Which is a treat. Sometimes I think what I do, running around trying to help people, shortchanges the people I love the most. I mean there's hardly a night goes by when there ain't somebody sitting down eating with us or knocking at the door or calling on the telephone for this or that.

I'm thinking about this and all the other things I found out that day, so when I finally hear Mary talking to me and says "What?" she says, "You were a million miles away."

"No, I wasn't. I was maybe a couple of miles and forty years from here."

"That's more than a million miles. What did you find out today?"

"Well, for one thing, I found out that Goldie Hanrahan had a child."

Mary gives a little gasp and leans forward, all ears, because all of a sudden Goldie ain't just this woman from another generation what got herself killed by misadventure or some other way, she's a mother just like Mary's going to be. Thats what women got going for them that men ain't got, this connection to one another because they give life.

"When?"

"Back in '50, '51."

"Wartime," Mary says.

"Wartime sure enough even if they did call it a police action," I says.

"Was the father a soldier?"

I think about the picture of my old man in uniform, squinting against the sun on the boardwalk in Atlantic City, with his arm around Goldie's waist and a grin on his face like he was doing what a man going off to war should be doing his last days—and nights—at home.

"I don't know was he a soldier. I don't know nothing about him. I just know that Goldie Hanrahan had a baby when she was sixteen, maybe seventeen, and a few years after that she gets a job with the city."

Mary's face gets sad and maybe a little mad, too. "What are you saying, James? Did somebody pay her off with a job instead of a wedding ring?"

"I don't know that, either. But the timing and all makes it a possibility."

"What do you mean 'and all'?" Mary asks.

"She kept the baby until it was about five and then she gives it to her mother or maybe her sister to raise."

"That happens all the time, James. It's not easy for a single working mother." She sits back in her chair, leans her elbow on the back of it, turns her head away, and puts her knuckle up to her lips. She's quiet for a long time, then she sighs and turns back to the table and me.

"Where's Goldie's child now?"

"Her child would be older than me."

"Are you going to try finding him?"

"I don't know. I don't know if it's any of my business. Besides, if her mother took it, she'd be dead by now and couldn't tell me what happened to her grandson."

"But the sister would know even if she didn't take it in herself."

I just nod.

"You going to look?"

"I suppose I am. I'm going to look because I got a notion that her having a boy almost forty years ago may have had something to do with her death the other day."

"What makes you think that?"

"You'd be surprised the secrets people keep and the way they keep them. Goldie Hanrahan started out working class in the Tenth. Some of the girls come out of there became whores and some became nuns, and some got married to steelworkers like their fathers and some got out of the neighborhood one way or another. Only a few ever climbed as high as Goldie Hanrahan, but rich or poor, whore or nun, I don't think the neighborhood ever left any of them.

"Goldie had a fancy apartment in a high-rise but she had a room in the apartment that was made up to look like the room she probably had when she was sixteen years old. A single bed, a chair, and a dresser with a mirror and some pictures of boyfriends on it."

Mary's not saying anything. She knows there's going to be more. The phone rings.

I start to get up.

"Let it ring," Mary says.

But I got to answer it because if I don't I got to tell Mary about the picture of my old man and Goldie and somehow I don't want to do that.

"Hello," I says into the phone. "Jimmy Flannery here."

"This is Marilyn O'Connell. Mr. Carrigan's secretary."

"Sure, I remember who you are, Ms. O'Connell," I says, glancing over to Mary.

She's getting the funny look on her face like she did the other night at supper when she got mad at me when I said Carrigan threw this redheaded secretary at my head. I'm standing there thinking if I pretend that Marilyn O'Connell was somebody else and Mary worms the truth out of me, then it'll look like something's going on that I'm trying to be sly about. So here I am letting her know up front that it's Marilyn O'Connell I'm talking to but she's getting mad at me anyway. It's hard to figure women out sometimes.

"Are you listening to me, Mr. Flannery?" Marilyn O'Connell says.

"Sure I am, Ms. O'Connell," I says.

"Well, you certainly aren't acting very concerned about it."

"About what, Ms. O'Connell?" I says, using her name each and every time to show Mary that our relationship is not only casual but strictly business. Which seems to be working because Mary's face is losing that look. "You'll have to run the train by me one more time."

"Well, I never," she says. "I just told you that Mr. Carrigan knows that your mutt had his way with Mistinguette."

"With his what?"

"His prize bitch," she practically shouts.

"Jesus, Mary, and Joseph," I says.

"You're going to need them."

"How'd he find out?"

"I didn't tell him, if that's what you're thinking, Mr.

Flannery. But somebody did. Mr. Carrigan's got eyes and ears all over the place. You should know that."

"Oh, I do," I says. "I do."

"Well, I just thought I'd tell you."

"It was nice of you."

"I've heard a lot about how you slip and slide, Mr. Flannery." She gives a little giggle. "I just think it's going to be fun to see how you squeeze out of this one."

• 16 •

I GOT OTHER THINGS to worry about than a pregnant dog. I got a pregnant lady from forty years ago to worry about.

I go back to the notes I wrote down from Goldie's appointment book.

I still ain't got a clue about this "Shedd, B.B.?"

I got the three numbers for the Johns, Markowitz, MacNamara, and Milholland. I dial them one by one.

The first one's a lawyer, the second one's a construction firm, and the third one's an old man in a nursing home who can't come to the phone, this lady tells me, because he's had a fall and ain't feeling well.

I'm ready to bet on the attorney.

I call up Markowitz again. This time I ask his receptionist if I can speak to him.

"What is the nature of your business?" she asks.

"Well, it's confidential, you know what I mean?" I says.

"I'm his confidential secretary," she says with a little

smirk in her voice, "so if you'll tell me the nature of your business, it might save a considerable amount of your valuable time."

I don't see how me telling her anything is going to save me any time at all, except if I don't tell her, I'll never get anywhere.

"It concerns a client of his," I says. "A Ms. Goldie Hanrahan."

"One moment," she says, and cuts me off.

A minute later a man's on the phone. "Who's this?" he says.

"My name's Jimmy Flannery," I says. "Is this Mr. Markowitz?"

"What about Ms. Hanrahan?" he says, not answering my question. Not being polite.

"Have I got the right John Markowitz? Do you represent Ms. Goldie Hanrahan?"

"I represent a Ms. Florence Hanrahan," he says, making it clear that he ain't going to use the nickname of a client with somebody on the phone he don't know and ain't got any ideas about.

This tells me that he's a very cautious man.

"I never knew her name was Florence," I says.

"Well, then," he says, as though that settles my status as a friend or even an acquaintance. "Just how can I be of service?" he goes on, like he don't really want to be of any service at all.

"I can tell you're a good lawyer," I says, "the way you go pussyfooting around, not giving even a little bit of nothing away. I want to talk to you about the Ms. Hanrahan who died recently."

"I'm well aware of that."

"I don't doubt it. What I'd like to talk about is how come you was on her appointment list the morning she died."

"Yes?"

"I'd like to know if she ever canceled that appointment. I'd like to know what it was going to be about."

"I really don't see that it's any of your business, Mr. —ah—Fredericks was it?"

"Flannery. Jimmy Flannery."

"I must point out to you that what transpires between a client and her attorney is privileged, even if inquired after by someone or some agency with authority. You have no official status that I know about."

"Oh, then you know who I am?"

"How's that?"

"If you know I ain't official, then you know who I am and all that misremembering my name was just playing power games. Right?"

"Mr. Flannery—"

"No, no. That's what you're doing or you're stalling for time while you think about what I'm asking you to do. I'm asking you to see me for ten, maybe fifteen, minutes. Let's just say I'm an old friend of Goldie's—"

"Who didn't know her name was Florence," he butts in with a little self-satisfied purr like he was a cat what got the mouse.

"Be that as it may, I know Goldie from way back and even if we wasn't bosom buddies, I got the ear of lots of important men that was. Some of them would maybe want to know why her attorney don't want to cooperate by answering a couple questions could maybe help clear up her murder."

"Murder!" he yelps like I stepped on his tail.

"It's a possibility."

There's a pause while I let my last remark sink in. I got the feeling that somebody important did, indeed, tell him to clam up about Goldie Hanrahan in case anybody should ask, but Markowitz never figured on concealing evidence in a murder case. So I can practically hear him wondering if he can split the difference, if by talking to me it'll keep his promise to whoever and keep me from maybe going to the cops and blowing the whole thing wide open. Obviously he don't know that my relations with the cops ain't the most cordial.

"You want to talk on the phone or you want me to come on over?" I asks. "If you really don't know nothing about me, it'll give you a chance to check me out."

"How long will it take you to get here?"

"Say twenty minutes."

"Very well."

"When you check up on me, it's okay if you ask anybody with political connections—like Ray Carrigan's a good bet—but I'd just as soon you don't check with the cops."

"Oh, why is that, Mr. Flannery?" he asks, like I just proved every bad thought he's been having about me.

"Because what we're doing is not official," I says, letting him know that no matter what he chooses to tell me I'll never reveal the source.

I'm at his office in fifteen minutes. Even so the attitude is very different, very cordial.

The receptionist shows me into Markowitz's office with a big smile and the offer of a cup of coffee.

Markowitz gets up from his chair and reaches across his desk to shake my hand and offer me a seat.

"You checked up on me?" I says.

"I made one or two calls."

"So I'm okay with you?"

"I'd say so. I'd say that at least I believe you mean Ms. Hanrahan or her reputation no harm."

"Did you call her Ms. Hanrahan?" I asks.

"No."

"Florence?"

"No, I called her Goldie, just like everybody else."

"So since we was both friends, at least old acquaintances, can we stop talking about Ms. Hanrahan?"

He studies me for a New York second.

"You're a friendly man, aren't you, Mr. Flannery?" he says.

"My old man always says you can catch more flies with sugar that you can with vinegar, and everybody calls me Jimmy."

"All right, let it be Goldie and Jimmy and Jack," he says, poking himself in the chest with his thumb. "Are you trying to catch flies, and what fly are you trying to catch, Jimmy?"

"I don't know. I don't know do we have here a death by misadventure or—"

"You called it murder."

"I think that's_a possibility. I got to know a few things. Maybe you can tell me a few things?"

The receptionist brings me a cup of coffee. Nothing for Markowitz.

"It sours my stomach," he explains, not wanting me to think he's being a bad host not having a cup with me.

Then he swivels in his chair, six inches this way, six inches that way, puckering up his lips and steepling his fingers while he watches me take a swallow of coffee. Working it out in his head how much he should tell me.

I decide to give him a little nudge.

"Goldie want to talk to you about her kid?"

His eyes open a little wider for a minute and he stops swiveling. "You know about her son?"

I just nod my head.

"Then you know more than practically anybody else, except me," he says.

"And the son and a couple of relatives and maybe the father."

"That goes without saying."

So now I know the father from forty years back is in the know about the son coming back, which means Goldie told him because she was the only one who knew who the father was.

And maybe Markowitz knows if she trusted him enough and she needed someone to confide in. So if anybody had anything to do with Goldie's death it could be the man what gave her the kid then walked out on her.

"You happen to know the name of the father?"

He shakes his head no.

"Goldie didn't tell me everything," he says.

"How much of what she told you are you willing to tell me?"

He thinks about that.

"Jack," I says, "you've had all the time in the world to check me out and to think about how you want to handle this. Maybe I'm just a buttinsky. Maybe I just spend my time sticking my nose into other people's business. Maybe I'm some kind of freak likes to poke through dead women's underwear drawers. But I doubt if that's the word you got on me. I can understand your natural caution. It's what they teach you in law school and I admire a pair of tight lips as much as the next guy, but ain't I right when I say that if you took my advice and called Ray Carrigan, he told you it was okay to give me what you got? Now even if you called somebody else—the somebody who told you sometime or other to clam up if Jimmy Flannery came around—"

"No one ever—" he starts to say.

"Sure they did. There's no reason to lie to me about that. You wasn't going to talk to me—"

"Client-attorney confidentiality."

"—until I mentioned the possibility of murder and then you can see it maybe wouldn't be so good to try and stonewall me just because this other person said so."

"Oh, all right," Markowitz says, "you could be right."

"So then you know that I'm going through this whole exercise because somebody asked me to do the favor."

"All right," he says, the way people do when they've made up their mind to stop playing games and get down to the nitty. "Goldie came to me with her secret about three months ago. She told me she was indiscreet when very young and became pregnant as a consequence. I responded by telling her that I was not the proper person to offer such a confession, that she'd do better consulting her priest. She said that she wasn't ashamed before God for what happened since it was God who gave young men and women the desire, then threw them together and told them to multiply."

"That sounds like Goldie. She had a clear eye and a wise heart—God rest her soul."

"She told me her concern wasn't religious, nor even moral. It might be legal. Beyond that, what she did about the situation would say something about her own integrity. But she also wanted to make certain she wasn't being victimized."

"Somebody approaches her claiming to be the son she gave to her mother or sister to raise and she ain't sure it's really him?"

"Who told you about the mother and sister?"

"An old friend of hers by the name of Sissy Palou."

"Well, she had it partly right. The mother couldn't take the baby when Goldie decided she had to give it up. The sister said she'd take the boy."

"And Goldie'd visit?"

"And pay its way. That's right. And she did visit. Every week. Then the sister's husband wanted to locate in another state where there were better job opportunities. He was a steelworker and the local mills were going through the bad times they went through before they went out of business altogether. So the sister said that Goldie either took the kid back or she'd have to travel to Pennsylvania to see it."

"Goldie said okay to that?"

"What could she say? is the way she put it when she told me about it."

"How often did she make the trip?"

"Once, sometimes twice a year for about two, three years."

"And?"

"She missed a couple of years. That was the last she saw of the boy."

I wait for what comes next.

"The sister died when Goldie's son was nine. The boy was taken in by another couple. The husband—Goldie's brother-in-law—went looking for work and later disappeared."

"None of that sounds very clear to me. Didn't Goldie know about her sister's death?"

"There'd been some sort of quarrel between them the last time Goldie went to visit her son. Something about Goldie flying high and the sister breaking her back raising Goldie's kid along with her own."

"How many kids did she have?"

"Two. A boy and a girl."

"Older or younger than Goldie's kid?"

"Older. The boy was about twelve when Goldie's kid was about seven, at the time of the last visit. The girl was maybe a year or two older than her brother."

"So what happened to them? They go with the father?"

"The boy might have. The girl had run off just before the mother died."

"Would either one of them know who adopted Goldie's boy?"

"Not adopted. Sheltered. Taken in. The boy might, if we knew where to look for him. He would've been about fourteen when the family disintegrated. Maybe he took off on his own. It happens every day."

"And Goldie's brother-in-law?"

"Still alive if the evidence Goldie had in her purse was to be believed."

"What was that?"

"A postcard."

"Could I get a look at that postcard?"

He reaches into the desk drawer and brings out the object in question. He hands it to me.

There's a colored picture of Miami Beach on the front. The postmark's from Sarasota. All it says is: "Hi there, Goldie. Here's a voice from the past. What a surprise, huh? What's it been, thirty years since I wrote to tell you Mabel died??? I'm sorry things happened the way they happened. I didn't know what else to do!!! Anyway your kid came to see me wanting to know about his real mother. Don't ask me why he wants to know at this late date. He must be nearly forty. I didn't know if you wanted to see him but he said he had a right and what could I say??? So whatever happened happened and no sense crying over spilt milk. Your brother-in-law, Ed. P.S. Should I say ex-brother-in-law? P.P.S. The people who took Charlie in was named Shedd so that's his name too. P.P.P.S. I'll be in Chicago around Thanksgiving. You want to talk to me I'll be at the La Salle Motor Lodge. You want to talk to Charlie I'll set it up."

I take out the appointment book I got from Goldie's apartment.

"What's that you got there?" Markowitz asks, but before I can tell him he adds, "Scratch that. I don't want to know."

"Then I'll just tell you Goldie had an appointment with a Shedd, B.B., with a question mark, scheduled early the morning she died. I don't know if she wrote down her itinerary in order, but if she did, the date with Shedd came before the breakfast with this old friend I mentioned, Sissy Palou. You say Goldie's kid's last name was Shedd and the first name Goldie gives him was Charlie?"

"Charles—Charlie—that's right."

"I wonder if his foster family changed his first name, too. Goldie's got B.B. with a question mark, down here."

Markowitz clears his throat like it's suddenly filled up.

"All the while she was telling me her story about her kid she kept on calling him Baby Boy," he says.

"So Baby Boy with a question mark. I guess Goldie had her doubts about that."

· 17 ·

AN HOUR LATER we're still talking, Markowitz and me. But we've already left his office and gone over to this saloon where we sit in the back booth while Markowitz has a draft and I have a ginger ale and we both dip into a bowl of bar fries.

He tells me that Goldie goes to have a talk with this brother-in-law. Her kid's uncle.

"Ed?"

"That's right. Ed."

"Ed what?"

"Ed Sickle."

"How'd she say it went?" I asks.

"Well, she said the obvious. A lot of years had passed. He didn't look much like she remembered him. He'd lost his teeth and wasn't wearing his dentures because he told her his gums were sore. He'd lost a lot of weight. He was shorter than she remembered him. He'd lost a lot of hair and grown a beard."

"So what was she saying?"

"What?"

"I mean was she convinced this guy was her brother-in-law?"

"Certainly. They talked about her sister and how she died. Then he told her about putting the boy with these friends. What kind of people the Shedds were. How good they were to Charlie."

"This was back around '58, '59?"

"About then."

"And nobody tried to tell Goldie that Ed Sickle was giving her kid away?"

"Goldie told me that Ed claimed he wrote to her right after her sister's death but she never answered, and that made him mad at the time and he thought the hell with her. She says she never got the letter if he really did send a letter."

"When did she find out about her sister dying?"

"About two years after that. She made the effort to try to make it up because she wanted to see Charlie again. Apparently whoever was living in the house opened her letter to her sister by mistake and after they read it, decided to write her back and tell her what they'd been told had happened to the sister and the boy they'd called Charlie and the husband, Ed, who'd taken off God knew where."

"So the Shedds weren't living next door with Charlie anymore?"

"They were apparently long gone and the new tenants in her sister's house didn't know where they'd gone either."

I think about the whole business while Markowitz orders another bowl of bar fries.

"Wait a second," I finally says. "Are you telling me that Goldie told you she'd gone to visit her kid for two, three years, then missed a year, a couple of years—it could happen—because she has a fight with her sister and the sister dies, but Goldie don't find out about it until a couple years after that when she also finds out the brother-in-law gives the kid away to some people what move away, and Ed Sickle takes off also and nobody don't even stay in touch?"

"It happens."

"The Shedds got this kid what don't even belong to the person what gives it to them and they don't even stay in touch?"

"I could tell you stories."

"And Goldie don't keep in touch—even if we give her the benefit she can't go see her kid because she's in Chicago a thousand miles away from Pennsylvania—for two more years after her sis dies? What's going on here?"

"Time flies," Markowitz says. Then he makes a face and adds, "I didn't mean that to be funny. I just meant it gets away from us along with all our best intentions."

"So all right. Now Goldie finds out her sister's dead and her kid's with strangers and where's the brother-in-law? Where's Ed Sickle? You tell me he disappears?"

"The people who wrote her the letter said that he left Pennsylvania looking for work elsewhere."

"And leaves the kid with these neighbors."

"That happened before. They'd already left the neighborhood."

"So tell me about these people."

"The Shedds were friends and next-door neighbors of the Sickles. They had no children of their own. The wife in particular doted on Charlie. So did her husband for that matter.

"When Ed's wife died and he couldn't take care of the boy on his own, he just let the Shedds take the boy in. He told people he wasn't exactly *giving* his nephew away. At first it was just an informal arrangement. Charlie would visit next door and stay for supper. Then he started sleeping over. After a year or so the boy was at the Shedds' more than he was at the uncle's. That was the gossip in the neighborhood that these new tenants heard about and wrote to Goldie about."

"How about Sickle's own kids?"

"The girl had run off already when she was thirteen or fourteen."

"Why?"

"Goldie said she'd always been wild. They couldn't manage her even when she was a toddler."

"Nothing funny with the father or the brother and the girl?"

"There could've been. The family sounds the type."

"What type is that?"

"Careless. Casual. Uneducated. Financially distressed."

"So people who're well off don't have trouble with fathers fooling with daughters, brothers fooling with sisters?"

"Hold the phone," Markowitz says. "Don't get mad at me. I'm not making a social comment here. I'm not sending down any class indictments. You asked me for my impression. All right, I shouldn't've answered you. I don't know these people. I never met them. All I know about them is what Goldie told me. In my way of thinking the brother-in-law sounds like the kind might've had knowledge of his daughter. His son may have been fooling around with his sister, too. I'm just saying maybe that's why she ran away. The point is she ran away and she can't help us in any way, shape, or form."

"Her brother?"

"Earl? Ditto. He split as soon as he was old enough. With his mother dead and his sister gone, I guess there was no reason for him to stay with the father."

"Hey, I'm sorry. I didn't mean to bite your head off

like that. I don't know why I did that except my wife's having a baby and I notice I've been acting very nervous lately, feeling a little sick in the morning, you know what I mean? Getting touchy. I mean, here I ask you a question and when you give me an answer I bite your head off. I eat all the time, too. Look at me, I must've gobbled up three-quarters of these two bowls of fries."

"That's okay. When my wife got pregnant I didn't get any morning sickness but I ate like a horse. It's nerves and worry that does it."

"Well, so Goldie has this talk with the brother-in-law and what does he tell her about her kid?"

"You understand the kid would be—let me see—almost forty, maybe thirty-eight or -nine. Ed tells Goldie that maybe two years ago he gets a call from Sheila Shedd."

"How'd she run Ed down?"

"It was one of those things. Her husband—Mike Shedd'd been a steelworker, too. They were in the same union and hung around the same local hall and pool-rooms. Ed Sickle came back to Pennsylvania after knocking around the country for years. Anyway, he was back in Pennsylvania and stopped into the old hangouts and met some old friends who were also friends of Mike Shedd. Mike Shedd died before they could get together, but it was then that Sheila Shedd called Ed and invited him to the funeral. She told him that Charlie was coming in from New Jersey for the funeral but he hadn't arrived yet. They sat there in the funeral parlor talking about the old days like people do, and she told him that they'd never tried to keep it secret from Charlie that he wasn't their own child."

"Does that mean that Charlie thought Mabel and Ed Sickle was his real parents?"

"No, he remembered his mother. He remembered Goldie but only vaguely. At the funeral parlor he blamed

Ed for him turning out useless the way he had. They had a knock-down, drag-out fight right there in the slumber room with the corpse of Mike Shedd lying ten feet away. There were no punches thrown, but Ed told Goldie it almost came to that. He said he managed to get Charlie outside for a smoke and told him if Charlie wanted to blame anybody for not doing right by him he should blame Goldie Hanrahan, his mother, who'd become a very important woman in Chicago and was probably still living there in the lap of luxury. Also she might be able to tell him who his father was and he could go have a fight with him."

"So?"

"So Charlie told Ed he was going to go to Chicago and look up this Goldie Hanrahan and find out if Ed was a liar or not. Ed wasn't sure if he'd really do it, but he was coming back to Chicago on business so he had a long talk with Charlie, after he'd cooled down, and asked him if Charlie wanted him to set up a meeting with his mother instead of Charlie just walking in on her and maybe killing her with the shock of it."

"Which he did?"

"Which is what he was supposed to do."

"But you don't know if that meeting between Goldie and her kid ever took place?"

"I don't. I had an appointment with Goldie for after she met her son. If she was satisfied that he was who Ed said he was, she was going to change her will."

My head was filled up with all these things that were really secondhand, no more than hearsay.

"That your dog?" Markowitz asks, breaking into my thoughts.

I look down and Alfie's sitting there, eyeing the fry bowl.

"How'd you get out of the car?" I says.

"What kind of dog is that?" Markowitz asks.

"Just a mutt."

"I wondered. For a minute there I thought it was a Bouvier."

"What's that?"

"The Bouvier des Flandres. A very fancy breed. Very unusual."

"Do tell."

"Shall I order another bowl of fries?" Markowitz asks.

• 18 •

I HATE TO TELL YOU I said yes to the third bowl of fries and ate more than half of them. So I decide I ain't going to have any lunch.

Instead, I drive over to see if I can maybe have a talk with Goldie's dentist, Dr. Harry Slaughter.

His reception room don't look like a dentist's reception room, it looks more like a day school or a kindergarten with these crayon drawings pinned up all over the walls and a wastebasket in the corner what looks like a fat-bellied clown.

"Excuse me," I says to the pretty round-faced woman with very pink cheeks who's sitting behind the counter, "can you tell me if I got the right Dr. Slaughter?"

"Well, I don't think there's more than one Dr. Slaughter in the city, do you?" She giggles. "I mean that'd be too much. I mean the town'd be flooded with jokes about the dentists named Slaughter. As it is we get six or seven jokes a day. This isn't another joke, is it?"

"No, I'm just trying to find out if Dr. Slaughter was Ms. Florence Hanrahan's dentist."

The happy smile blinks off her face. "Goldie. Oh, dear. I read about it in the papers. I heard it on the news. What a thing to happen."

The smile comes back. She's got the kind of face a smile can't stay away from for long.

"Well, at least she was doing something she loved to do in a place she loved," she says.

"Oh? What do you know about Saganashkee Slough and Goldie Hanrahan?"

She leans forward like what she's about to tell me is very confidential.

"It had romantic connotations," she whispers.

"Would you run that train by me one more time?"

"Ms. Hanrahan was never married but she was a very romantic woman."

She says that like she knows because she's a very romantic woman, too.

"She told me stories about when she was young. Nothing indiscreet, mind you. Just lovely stories about how she used to meet her beaus here and there, in places that were out of the ordinary. Out of the city. In the country. She told me how she sometimes drove out to the forest preserve with a special boyfriend and parked by a lake. She called it a lake but it was the Saganashkee Slough. She told me this special boyfriend taught her to ride horseback out there at Saganashkee Slough."

The smile goes away again and she asks me if my business with Dr. Slaughter concerning Goldie Hanrahan is official.

I says that I'm making discreet inquiries but I don't say for who.

The door to the treatment rooms opens up and this little man in a white coat, with a face just as round and cheeks just as pink as his receptionist's, comes out holding the hand of a little boy with a gap-toothed grin. A young woman, who I suppose is the kid's mother, is smiling to beat the band.

Dr. Slaughter smiles at his receptionist, who smiles back.

"Maggie, two balloons for my friend, Joey, here."

Maggie blows up two balloons with helium stored in a small tank sitting by her desk which you couldn't tell was a tank until she blows up the balloons because it's dressed like a clown.

Slaughter hands the balloons to Joey, who takes them in his pudgy fist, then gives the dentist a hug.

Joey and his mother toddle out the door and Slaughter turns to me.

"I wish I had a dentist like you when I was a kid," I says.

"How about now?" he says. "You got a dentist?"

I don't answer right away.

"When was the last time you had your teeth cleaned?"

"Well, last—maybe a year—I don't know—could be two years." I'm stuttering like I used to stutter when I was in the fifth grade and Mrs. Prager caught me squirting Virginia Whitely at the water fountain or running up and down the stairs.

Maggie's shaking her head and going, "Tch, tch, tch," like I'm really the worst case of dental neglect they've heard about in a long time.

"Well, come along in and let me have a look."

"I'm afraid this gentleman hasn't got an appointment," Maggie says.

"Oh." He thinks a second, trying to look serious even though he's got this face that seems to be smiling even when his mouth ain't doing anything.

"I'll have a look anyway. You dropped in at just the right time."

"It's Doctor's lunch hour," Maggie says, like she's just

a little bit cross with me for keeping Slaughter from his eats.

"Begging your pardon," I says, managing to get a word in edgewise, "but I didn't come here to have my teeth examined."

"I understand. You dread the dentist. Not uncommon. Especially with people that were hurt by a dentist when they were small."

"Well, see, there you go. I'm not afraid of the dentist. So if I want to go to the dentist I don't have to go to one that takes care of little kids."

"That's what you say," Slaughter says, grinning at me like he don't believe a word I'm saying, and putting his hand on my shoulder.

He's pushing me toward the door and for some reason I find out that I'm letting him. I got no resistance.

"I'm not just a kiddie dentist, you understand," he goes on. "I've got as many adult patients as I've got children."

"Well, I can see you got a way with you," I says as he sits me down in the chair and Maggie bustles in to put a bib on me. "Was Goldie Hanrahan afraid of the dentist?"

His face does the same thing Maggie's face did when I mentioned Goldie's name.

"What a tragic accident," he says, picking up one of them little picks and a tiny mirror. "Put your head back and open wide, please."

"Did you make the bridge for Ms. Hanrahan?"

"Now," he says, and starts picking around inside my mouth while Maggie perches on a stool and writes down half of what he says—things like "third occipital surface" or something like that—onto a chart. That's the half about my teeth. The other half of what he says, sandwiched in here and there, is about Goldie's teeth.

"I constructed the partial that Ms. Hanrahan wore. . . .

A three on the anterior surface of the second molar. . . . She came to me with a mouth full of old crowns and fillings. Gold and amalgam scattered around all higgledy-piggledy. . . . Seven and four at the gumline, third incisor. . . . I excavated, shifted, reconstructed, and built a partial that was as comfortable as her own teeth had been. When she had them. She didn't take care of her teeth when she was young."

He leans back for a second and looks at me. The message he's giving me being I ain't doing a very good job on my teeth either. In that second, when there's nothing in my mouth, I says, "The bridgework is missing."

"Oh?"

"It could've flew out when she was knocked off her horse."

"Possible," he says.

"It could be laying out there in the underbrush alongside Saganashkee Slough."

"Uh-huh."

He's back at me with the pick and mirror. I open my mouth even though I ain't finished discussing what I come to discuss. Dentists got this funny thing about them; they get people to open their mouths just by sticking an instrument close to their face. Nobody hardly ever refuses.

"So you'd like to know more about the bridge in order to identify it should anyone ever come across it in the future? . . . Lower seven, eight, and nine filled with amalgam. Leaking. . . . That bridge'll be the easiest bridge in the world to identify."

He steps back again. It looks like he's finished picking at my teeth because he tosses the probe and mirror into a little pan.

"Rinse if you like," he says.

Maggie fills a little cup with pink stuff and I wash out, leaning over to spit in the bowl with the spiral of water squirting along the side, remembering the hundred times I sat in a dentist's chair and spit like that, bent over a bowl, glad that the whole torture was over.

"How's that?" I says.

"How's what?"

"How come the bridge'd be so easy to identify?"

"Goldie Hanrahan was a very romantic lady."

"So I've been told. Could you tell me why you say that?" I asks, giving Maggie the old one-eye, accusing her of gossiping to her boss about the girl talk she had with Goldie.

"Some of her fillings," Slaughter says.

"Who's the one pulling teeth around here?" I says.

He looks dumb for a second, then they both start to laugh.

"That's a good one," Slaughter says. "Well, okay, what I mean is that Goldie asked me to replace a few of her fillings with decorations."

I'm about to ask what kind of decoration is he talking about when he holds up a hand, asking me to hold my horses, opens a drawer, and comes out with a chart which he hands to me.

It's covered with all sorts of little designs, tiny flowers and hearts and butterflies, imbedded in plastic fillings.

"It was quite a fad there for a while," Slaughter says.

"See, I have a daisy," Maggie says, leaning her face toward me and pulling back her cheek with her finger so I can see this little daisy on the filling she's got in a back tooth.

"Beautiful," I says, not knowing what else to say.

"It's a novelty. But some women have it done for sentimental reasons."

"And that was the reason Goldie Hanrahan had it done?"

"I'd say so. She had me make three little initialed hearts, one for each tooth she wanted filled with the decorated plastic."

"Three?" I says. "That's really something. That's like the sailor who asked the tattoo artist what could he do about changing the name on a heart tattoo, and the tattoo guy said the best he could do was do another and the sailor could just tell the new girlfriend that the other one was for his mother. By the time this character got married he claimed that, besides a mother, he had thirteen sisters."

We have another laugh all around.

"Could you tell me the initials on the teeth?" I asks.

"I'd have to look it up."

"Would you?"

He looks doubtful.

"It's only initials," I says. "You ain't giving nothing away that could hurt Goldie."

"It might hurt someone else. Just what is it you want, Mr. . . . ?"

"Flannery, Jimmy Flannery," I says.

Maggie writes it down on my chart.

"What is it you're after?" Slaughter asks again.

"I'm not saying Goldie Hanrahan's death wasn't an accident," I says. "I'm saying that just in case it turns out somebody killed her and stole her bridgework because he was afraid it'd put the finger on him, I'd like to know who that somebody is."

"I don't suppose you're with the police or you'd have identified yourself."

"No, I'm not. I'm just a friend trying to do right by a friend what ain't around anymore to defend herself. Now you can take my word for it or not. That's up to you."

"And if I choose not to take your word?"

"I'll tell the cops what I found out so far and they'll

ask you the same questions I'm asking you, which could mean maybe they'll do something with it, maybe they won't."

"All right," he says, making up his mind quick.

Maggie goes out.

"Your teeth are actually in pretty bad shape," Slaughter says.

"Please don't say that."

"Not the worst I've ever seen, but pretty bad. You've got half a dozen cavities starting and some periodontal work needs doing. I think we should arrange a series of appointments."

"I don't know."

"It's up to you. I'm not out to hustle another customer. I have plenty. Think about it and just remember this: When I say I'm a painless dentist, that doesn't mean there won't be a little twinge now and then, but I'm very, very good at what I do and very, very careful about what I promise, if I do say so myself."

"I believe you. I saw Joey out there."

"There you are."

Maggie comes back with Goldie's records. Slaughter looks through them and finds the page.

"The initials were B.B., R.C., and M.F."

Baby Boy? Ray Carrigan? Mike Flannery?

• 19 •

ALL MY LIFE, whenever I got a problem, I always go to my old man to talk it over. Not that he always comes up with any useful answers, but if nothing else, he usually asks so many questions or causes such an argument it makes me get it straight in my head what I'm really worried about and what I'm going to do about whatever.

But this time I got a problem which I don't see how I can go to my old man about it. I mean if Goldie Hanrahan's got these sentimental little hearts buried in her fillings and one of them you can figure stands for Baby Boy, which is how she thinks of her lost son, Charlie, then I got to figure the other sets of initials are in memory of a couple of people for which she kept a special place in her heart.

Now a lady what was a beauty—a heart-stopper when she was young—probably had more boyfriends than a ward heeler could hope for supporters in a close election. Goldie was not known to be a shrinking violet or a woman dedicated only to her work.

She was very discreet about her affairs and also very discreet about her memories and very discreet about mementos of same, otherwise she wouldn't have put the initials in her fillings but would've had them tattooed on one of the hidden places where ladies put such things.

There had to be a reason why she picked on R.C. and M.F. out of all the men she'd known. And it didn't take a genius of a detective from the Twenty-seventh to figure out that one or the other or both of them had something to do with Baby Boy. Like one of them was the father but there was some confusion about which one.

I also got to take the shot—knowing the cast of characters, the time sequence, and the probable scene where it all took place—that R.C. stands for Ray Carrigan. The next question is does M.F. stand for Michael Flannery, which I already said is a very good bet.

So that's how come I didn't see any way I could talk the whole thing over with my old man unless I wanted to come right out and ask him was he possibly the father of the late Goldie Hanrahan's forty-year-old Baby Boy.

Which don't mean that I'm without resources for consultation.

Since I been married to Mary Ellen Dunne I got somebody who if anything is even smarter than my old man, who knows when I'm just batting the ball around without expecting anything more than a backboard and who don't take the wrong side of an argument just for the hell of it the way Mike does. At least not until lately.

Lately, being pregnant like she is, you can't always be

sure what reaction you're going to get to anything you do.

But I got to talk to somebody, Alfie being bored with the whole business so far as I can tell. Maybe things that happened so far in the past ain't really very important to a dog.

"I know you got your own worries, Alfie," I says. "We could both end up being fathers, though it ain't exactly the same thing, Mary and me being married."

He's laying down in his place on the passenger side of the front seat, his head on his paws, but he lifts his head enough to give me the old one-eye.

"I'm not saying marriage has the same importance in a dog's life, but no matter how you slice it, this here Mistinguette is in a family way and you got to admit you done it without nobody's permission."

He barks.

"Mistinguette excepted, of course."

I park the car in front of the apartment house and I ain't walked three steps when Shirley Shapiro stops me.

Shirley and her husband, Myron, live on the second floor. She's a librarian and he's a teacher.

When Mary and me decide to buy the building to keep it from being knocked down instead of building a house on the lot Mrs. Banjo, Delvin's housekeeper, left us in her will, the Shapiros, along with the other tenants, scraped up what pennies they had and put it in the pot.

So Mary and me own the biggest piece of the property but everybody's got an interest in remodeling it, keeping it nice, and sharing expenses.

"Jimmy," Shirley says, "Myron and I decided we'd like to tear out a wall and put in a two-person whirlpool tub in the bathroom."

"That sounds good to me, Shirley, except ain't that going to make the living room a lot smaller than you maybe would like it?"

"We're pushing back the dining room eight feet."

"That would make it about as wide as a hallway."

"That's right. If we shift the back bedroom door from the wall it's in now to the new wall, the old dining room will be like a hallway which will open up to the kitchen. So we can have it like a kitchen and dining room together. What they call a harvest kitchen."

"I look at the magazines, too, Shirley, and if I remember right, a harvest kitchen works if you got about twice the space you got for a kitchen."

"Not if you eliminate the dining room."

"So that's your idea?"

"I want to know if you think it's something we should bring up at the owners' meeting or if we can just go ahead and do it since the apartment is, after all, ours."

"Well, it's yours and nobody can raise your rent without your say-so or kick you out unless you make so much noise you scare old Mrs. Foran's cat, but it sounds like a major alteration which some people might think would detract from the value of the building."

"Add to it, Jimmy. Add to it."

"Well, if you're asking my opinion, I'd bring it up at the owners' meeting."

She makes a little face and says, "I was afraid you were going to say that."

"Why was you afraid?"

"You know how Myron is. He hates to have to ask permission to do anything."

I know Myron. He's the easiest-going man you'd want to meet and practically asks your permission to pass you in the hall. It's Shirley who likes to have her own way and hates asking anybody if she can do anything, but I just nod and smile and let her know how much I sympathize with her for all she has to put up with with Myron.

I go on upstairs with Alfie at my heels. He scratches on the door while I'm trying to get my key out. I hear Mary's feet, wearing slippers, come padding into the hall and she opens the front door. Alfie makes a big fuss and she gives him a pat.

I stick my tongue out like I'm panting and make like a dog. She pats me, too, and says, "If the people down at city hall could see you acting so silly they'd wonder if Carrigan did the right thing naming you the committeeman for the Twenty-seventh."

"When did you hear that?"

"About half an hour ago. Mr. Delvin called. He wanted to be the first to tell you, but since you weren't here he said it was okay if I did the honors."

"Honors," I says.

"You don't act overjoyed," Mary says, following me out to the kitchen where I sit down because all of a sudden my feet hurt and I'm feeling very weary.

"What's the matter, James, don't you feel well?"

"Just a little tired."

"I'm the one who's supposed to be feeling tired."

She's got her head wrapped in an old scarf and she smells of soap so I know she's been going through the house again, cleaning from one end to the other even though she did it on her day off last week.

"It's all them steps. They take it out of me lately."

She comes over behind me and hugs me, then reaches down and pats my stomach. "Got to do something about that," she says. "People will think you're the one that's pregnant. You want a cup of tea?"

"That'd be good."

While she's putting the water on and getting out the pot, she's giving me the eye.

"Don't you care about your appointment, James?"

"Who are we kidding, Mary? People been telling me for years that the machine's rusted and busted and I always act like a fool pretending that it ain't. The courts took the clout out of patronage a long time ago. So maybe it was a bad thing sometimes but I don't know it was any worse hiring friends and relatives than having useless people in civil service you have a hell of a time getting out, no matter what. Besides, people can't do favor for favor one way, they'll figure out how to do it another. It probably works out the same.

"Also the mix of people in the neighborhoods is changing. I'm a generation younger but I guess I'm like the old rhinos and elephants, Carrigan and Dunleavy and Delvin and even my old man, making believe it's like it was. I don't know should I be wasting my time in politics. I don't know if I make a difference anymore."

Mary sits down opposite me at the table and reaches across to take my hands.

"You make a difference, James. And I make a difference at Passavant. Maybe we don't make as big a difference as we did once upon a time. Maybe things have gotten too big for average people like you and me to make a big difference what with everything falling to pieces all around us. But they'd be falling to pieces a lot faster without us. So who cares what they call it? Ward politics or social welfare. Charity or entitlement. Favor for favor or a helping hand. It's all the same. Helping people and not crowing about it. Doing what you can to make things better and keeping your mouth shut about it."

The kettle starts to sing.

"That was a pretty good speech," I says.

"It's the one I hear you give every time somebody's ready to lie down in the sewer and drown."

Mary washes out the pot with boiling water, then tosses in a handful of tea leaves and pours fresh water over it to steep.

"By the way," she says, "Willy Dink called."

"What did he have to say?"

"He said he had some information for you about a pregnant bitch."

"Oh," I says.

"What's that all about?" Mary asks.

"You know Willy Dink. He gets some funny ideas."

Mary looks in the fridge and says, "Damn, we're out of lemons."

I jump up and says, "I'll run right on down to Joe and Pearl's and get a couple."

"Don't get to talking and stay an hour."

"I'll be back before the tea's ready to pour."

I hurry on downstairs and into the corner grocery store.

"Give me three lemons and let me use your phone."

"You have trouble with yours?" Joe asks.

"No," I says, looking at my watch. "I just this second remembered I had to call somebody and I got to catch him before he leaves where he's at."

Willy Dink lives in a van made for him on the back of an old Model A Ford truck by a wood butcher over in Cicero. It's a gorgeous piece of work in which he lives with his business partners or appliances—depending how you look at it. He's got this little creature what looks like an armadillo and likes to eat ants. He's got a chicken what gobbles up cockroaches and other bugs. Also he's got a rat terrier and a ferret, which he puts into the walls to eat the mice or drive them out. Also a snake for same.

He advertises hisself as "Willy Dink's Natural Vermin Control."

Since he's got no telephone in his van—which lately he's parking by Golbekian's Pool Hall over to the First—you can get him at Golbekian's, unless he's out on a job.

. I ring up the pool hall and get somebody what brings Willy Dink to the phone.

"Willy Dink's Natural Vermin Control," he says.

"This is Flannery," I says. "You got some news for me?"

"I check with my vet. He tells me there's no quicker way of telling is a bitch going to have puppies than to feel her belly about thirty days after you think some dog put her in a family way."

So that was that, I had to wait to find out if I was in trouble.

"The vet told me something else that might be of interest to you," Willy Dink says.

"What's that?"

"My vet tells me that a bitch can get pregnant by two different dogs and have a mixed bag of puppies."

"How close together do these two dogs have to meet up with the bitch?"

"Well, within a couple of hours, I guess. I didn't ask."

"I don't see how that'll do me any good," I says.

"Me neither, but I thought it was a useful piece of information in case you ever get into this pickle again and you want to spread some confusion."

I run back upstairs with the lemons just as Mary's pouring out the tea.

"You didn't have to run up those stairs," she says. "You're puffing like an old steam engine."

"I notice," I says, gasping for breath.

"You really should start thinking about losing a little weight. You notice Mike keeps himself in very good condition for a man his age."

"About Mike," I says.

"What about him?" Mary says, leaning toward me, knowing from the way I started that I got something worrisome to tell her.

"You know how it turns out Goldie Hanrahan has this baby out of wedlock forty years ago and nobody knew the father, and she gives it to her sister to raise but the next thing you know she loses touch and the sister dies, and the sister's husband gives the kid to neighbors and leaves the state and then the neighbors move someplace, too, and nobody knows where so Goldie don't even know where her kid ended up, except that it looks like he found out who she was and where she was just recently and maybe came to Chicago to look her up?"

"I'd say that sums up what you've told me so far, James."

"Well, there could be a strong possibility that my old man was the father of Goldie Hanrahan's child."

"Drink your tea, James," Mary says, "and tell me about it."

By the time I'm through telling Mary about why I think my father could've been one of maybe two men who was having what you'd call affairs with Goldie Hanrahan about the time she got pregnant, the second pot of tea is finished.

"Initials and tiny plastic hearts in her fillings? Who would've believed that the Goldie Hanrahan you told me ruled Ray Carrigan's office with an iron hand was that soft in her heart? Fancy having Baby Boy and the initials of two lovers put in your teeth?"

"Well, I read about these rock singers and movie actresses having tattoos put on places I won't mention, so I guess it ain't as nutty as it sounds."

"Now that we've talked it over," Mary says, "you know what you're going to do?"

"I'm going to dig around a little more."

"Sooner or later you're going to have to confront Mike with your questions and your feelings."

"I know, but right now I'd rather do it later than sooner."

· 20 ·

I'D LIKE IT if Mary'd quit working over to Passavant Hospital right now, but she says that'd be ridiculous. Here she is only three months pregnant and not even showing. What do I expect her to do, hang around the house with her feet up on the footstool, watching the soaps, reading trashy novels, eating chocolate and getting fat like me? I don't know why she has to make that last remark but I don't say nothing.

At least I got her to ask for days.

Anyway, she's not home when I get a telephone call the next morning.

You'd think with all the times you seen it on television and in the movies anonymous threats over the phone would've gone out of style. On the other hand if somebody wants to threaten or warn somebody else without letting on who they are, what other way could you use?

So I ain't too surprised when this rusty voice on the

other end of the wire says, "Flannery, why don't you mind your own business?"

"What business is that?" I asks.

"It's forty-year-old news. Fachrissake, who cares anymore?"

"Well, it looks like you, for one."

"I don't care. I'm just making a call for a friend."

"Look. You tell me the name of your friend and maybe I'll give it some consideration."

"Fachrissake you're as bad as they say. Can't you just take it like I delivered it and forget about the conversation?"

"I could do that, but the longer I keep you talking, the better chance I got to identify your voice, even though you're straining it through your sock."

He hangs up.

I sit there thinking about it. He's right. I'm digging into situations forty years old trying to find out how and maybe why Goldie Hanrahan got knocked off her horse and killed. If I was a bookie I'd be giving heavy odds against foul play. I'd be taking all the paper I could get from suckers betting it wasn't just a terrible accident.

So that leaves me with two ways to figure. Either the guy on the phone is really worried I'm going to dig up something that'll incriminate him in a murder or at the very least, in an illegitimate birth which—even though it happened forty years ago—could maybe cause some family problems today.

On the other hand it could be somebody—like Carrigan —who knows or suspects something me and the cops don't know and who's also worried I ain't taking the search for the true facts in the death of Goldie Hanrahan serious enough.

Knowing I got a reputation for being as mean and persistent as a junkyard dog when anybody tries to scare me off, he could figure there's nothing better for keeping

Flannery worrying the bone than telling him to cut it out.

I sit there over my second cup of coffee trying to sort out what I got.

I got a dresser in a fancy bedroom covered with pictures of powerful men in Chicago who was young when Goldie Hanrahan was young. Leaving out the state and national figures—though it don't necessarily mean it's out of the question one of them figures in it—I'm still left with more than a double handful of possibles.

Cutting it in even finer, considering just the pictures on the dresser in the plain little bedroom, I still got too many.

Possibles like Vito Velletri, who has dinner with the cardinal and once had an audience with the pope, and who's got a wife, children, and grandchildren he maybe figures could be upset or in some way injured if it turns out that he fathered a bastard by Goldie. So the kid appears after all these years to see his mother and maybe there's the chance that she tells him who his father is and that could lead to all kinds of things, including blackmail. So Velletri meets with Goldie in a spot where there's practically no chance of being seen so he can make sure she's still going to hold on to the secret. And somehow things get out of hand.

Then there's Smith Jarwolski, also married with kids and grandkids, who's also been making noises like a political candidate lately. Chances are, if young Daley gets into the mayor's chair, the party could run Jarwolski for state senate. He wouldn't be too happy to have an old indiscretion surface. Maybe he does something about it. But if he does something about it, why do it out in county jurisdiction? Why not keep it close to home where he could sit on it? Well, for one thing, him and

Koslow are old friends so it wouldn't be asking much for Koslow to sit on it for him.

My old Chinaman, Chips Delvin, is hardly a runner. For one thing he can hardly walk and for another thing there's nobody left alive from his own life who'd give a damn if he'd had a little go-round with Goldie forty years ago, no matter what came of it.

Ray Carrigan's a candidate, even though he's the one who's insisting I keep on it. Some people figure there's no better way to avoid suspicion than to go around yelling for an investigation. Look at Nixon not even bothering to burn the tapes while he's saying, "I'm not a crook." Look at Gary Hart asking for it the way he did. Also I notice that Carrigan ain't yelling at the cops or the sheriff's office to go all out. He's asking me, a private citizen.

So Carrigan's a possible. For one thing he's got so much pride he might even try to do something to somebody who threatened to tell the papers that Carrigan stole a candy bar from the five-and-dime when he was ten, let alone to somebody who threatens to tell the world he fathered a bastard and turned his back. You put together as many squeaky deals as Carrigan's put together and you get very touchy about how clean you keep your collars and cuffs.

Then there's Mike Flannery, my old man, and I don't want to think about is he capable of keeping the secret of a bastard son all these years, let alone doing somebody a serious injury.

But you figure in the initialed fillings and you got Ray Carrigan and Mike Flannery the odds-on favorites for being the father of her kid. On the other hand affectionate memories don't necessarily mean paternity.

And vice versa. Many a girl's had no special love for the guy what got her in a family way.

I decide to go at them one at a time, leaving Mike for last.

I tell Alfie to go get his leash, which he does, unhooking it from behind the door like I taught him, and we go down to get in the Chevy and get started.

Except these two panthers by the name of Ginger and Fink, which I've met many times before, mostly under neutral circumstances but once or twice when they let me know they'd bust my arms and legs if I didn't go along with them for a visit to Vito Velletri, are leaning against a big black sedan.

Since I'm going to see Velletri sooner or later I don't bother arguing, I just get in the back.

"Hey, not the dog," Ginger says.

"Alfie don't go, I don't go. What's the matter, you afraid he'll take a bite out of you?"

"Let him have the mutt," Fink says.

"I got to vacuum out the goddamn back seat," Ginger complains. "Dog hairs is hard to get off the upholstery."

"Keep the mutt on your lap," Fink growls.

I says okay and they get in the car and we drive over to Velletri's office in the Twenty-fifth.

Velletri's sitting behind this huge desk in his office, which is bigger and has got more wood, red velvet, and brass than the office of a corporation president or a church dignitary.

I been there once before when he wanted to know what I was doing nosing around his ward, and the place ain't changed very much.

He don't say anything about me carrying a dog into his office, he just says, "Sit down, Flannery," and waves a long, thin, pale hand at the leather chair on the other side from where he's sitting. "Glass of brandy?"

"No, thanks," I says, sitting down with Alfie on my lap.

"That's right, you don't drink very much."

He winces and puts a hand to his stomach. For a minute he goes whiter than he already is. He's pale as a ghost and thinned out like a shaved bone. His eyes are the eyes of man ninety, a hundred, even though Velletri's probably seventy-two, seventy-three. It looks to me that what I've been hearing around—that Velletri's got a cancer—could be true.

He reads my mind.

"It's an ulcer, not a cancer. I'll be around for a while," he says.

"I'm glad to hear that."

"Are you, Flannery? Are you really glad to hear that?"

"We had our differences and I never done much business with you, but I never wished bad luck on you."

"How about an espresso, then?" he asks.

"That'd be nice," I says.

"Ginger, bring Flannery an espresso and take his dog out and give him a drink of water, maybe a little hamburger."

Ginger gives me a dirty look but he takes Alfie from me and leaves the room.

"So what have you found out about Goldie Hanrahan's death?" Velletri asks.

"Just about nothing."

"What have you found out about Goldie Hanrahan?"

"She had a baby about forty years ago."

He nods.

"You knew about it?"

"She came to me for advice."

I try not to look surprised but I don't do a very good job of it or maybe he reads my mind again.

"She knew that I had strong religious feelings and many church connections. Maybe she wanted the counsel of a priest but was afraid to go to a priest so she came to me as the next best thing."

My first thought is that Velletri's got an angle and there's some benefit for him in this confession. Or maybe it's really a cancer not an ulcer he's got and he wants to make peace with his own soul for things he done in the past, though why he should pick me as the person to give him absolution escapes me. Or maybe he's ready to pay back some old debt or some old injury.

While I'm thinking all this he's watching me with the eyes of some ancient priest what reads minds and hearts.

"Don't think so much," he says "You don't have to think, I'm going to tell you. As soon as Ginger brings you your coffee."

Which happens that very minute like we're in a play and everything goes off right on cue. Ginger sets the cup and saucer down on the desk. There's even a little twist of lemon peel in the saucer along with a lump of sugar and a little silver spoon.

"Go somewhere," Velletri says. So Ginger and Fink leave us alone.

"We're talking here about 1951, '52. I'm thirty-two, -three years old, give or take a couple of years. I'm an older man to Goldie Hanrahan, you understand?"

I say I do but I don't.

"Your father's twelve, thirteen years younger than me. He's a soldier ready to go over to Korea and get his ass shot off."

"He come back okay."

"You mean he never got wounded? Well, he got wounded." He punches hisself in the chest with his thumb. "He was in love with Goldie Hanrahan. She was his girlfriend when he went off to war."

Somebody makes a sound like somebody's just been

punched in the belly. Then I realize that somebody's me.

"They was talking about getting married," Velletri goes on. "How do I know this? I was doing some leg-work for Ray Carrigan is how, looking the field over for potential leaders. Your father was on the list. Soon as he came out of the army—if he came out of the army—the Party was going to start grooming him."

"For precinct captain?" I says.

"For better than that. You're getting ahead of me. Drink your espresso. Here."

He reaches over and picks up the peel of lemon, gives it an expert little twist over the cup, and releases a drop of oil, then puts the twist back in the saucer and smells his fingers. "Lovely," he says, and watches me as I pick up the cup, without adding the lump of sugar, and take a sip. "Good?"

"Good," I says.

"Sure," he says, looking satisfied, as though a cup of espresso was the secret to the good life.

"He's not the only young guy we got our eye on. There's men like Ed Keady and Harry Winters and Marco Fenucci. There's also Smith Jarwolski. He don't go into the army. He's in the army right here in Chicago. He's a cop. He's going places. He's good-looking. He's tall. He wears a uniform. Women like uniforms."

"Goldie?"

"Some women is crazy about uniforms. Or maybe a girl—practically a kid—gets lonesome, you understand?"

I understand.

"Sure," he says, the same way he said it about the coffee.

"She went out with Jarwolski?"

"Many times. She also went out with other men.

They came around her like bees to honey. A beautiful young girl. Even I was smitten."

The old-fashioned word, dropping from his lips, which were like paper, sounded right, sounded okay.

"You understand I was a newly married man. My wife was going to have a baby. A man has a hunger."

"How many men were sleeping with Goldie Hanrahan?" I asks.

He straightens up a little bit. "I don't like the way you said that. Goldie was a friend of mine. Goldie was a beautiful young girl. She was in love with a man but he was a million miles away over somewhere. She works in the five-and-dime all day. At night what's she supposed to do—this beautiful young girl—stay home and watch the television?"

"If she was promised."

"I don't know about promises. You're an old man sometimes, Flannery. Older than me sometimes. You think everything's up or down, right or left, black or white."

"Promises don't have anything to do with young or old, right or left, black and white. Promises is promises. They keep us from falling off the edge of the world."

"She wasn't easy. You shouldn't think she was easy."

"Easy enough," I says. "There was my father and you and Smith Jarwolski and who else?"

"Not me. I just told you. The girl I found relief with was a girl named Sissy Palou."

"Who gave Goldie the baby?"

He opens his hands in a gesture that shows he's empty. He stares at me as though I just asked the question he'd been asking for forty years.

"She wouldn't say. That she wouldn't tell me. I told her I'd see to it he did the right thing. She said he already offered to do the right thing but she didn't want him to."

"If she didn't love the man enough to marry him, why'd she sleep with him?"

"Listen to you," Velletri says. "You know what everybody says about you, Flannery? People who like you and people who don't like you? They say, 'One thing about Flannery, he doesn't make judgments. He doesn't put anyone down for being human.' Listen to you judging Goldie Hanrahan with the way you talk."

He's right. I start to open my mouth but he puts up his hand like he's a traffic cop and cuts me off. "I understand. It's your father we're talking about. It's your father and the girl who could've ended up being your mother—in a manner of speaking."

"What did she want your advice about?"

"Should she have the baby, shouldn't she have the baby. If she didn't have it, she could live the lie and marry your father when he came home. That'd be that. She could live the life she was entitled to."

"And if she had it?"

"Go ask any single woman with a kid and no husband. It was even harder forty years ago."

"So you told her to go ahead and have the baby."

"I told her she'd come to the wrong person for advice. She'd come to an Italian Catholic whose own wife was going to have a child. How could I advise her to kill her child?"

I finished the espresso and sat there thinking about what he'd told me. Then I asked him why he'd told me.

"Because you've been digging around in Goldie's life and sooner or later you'd come across your father. I thought somebody should tell you how your father was involved with Goldie Hanrahan. I don't know everybody who might've been involved with her except the one I mentioned and maybe some others I don't mention because it doesn't matter anymore. I thought you might want to forget about this favor you're doing for Ray Carrigan."

"Why do you suppose he's so anxious to find out what happened to Goldie? Why won't he just accept the fact that she died by accident like Hackman says?"

"You'd have to ask that Irishman himself. I don't know how his mind works. Never did. Ask him was he a special friend of Goldie Hanrahan's back then. Ask him if he was another older man she went to for advice."

He lifts his chin and I take that to mean he's through with me, the interview's over. He's said all that he wants to say.

So I leave Velletri's office wondering what he told me. Did he tell me Smith Jarwolski was the father of Goldie's son? What exactly did he tell me?

• 21 •

I DRIVE OVER to the La Salle Motor Lodge, which ain't in the best section of town. It's a seedy old brick-and-stucco building with a couple of letters missing from the neon sign which spits as I go by it like an angry cat.

The owner, manager, whatever, behind the Formica counter in the plywood office ain't much friendlier. I get the feeling that anybody wearing a shirt and tie ain't really welcome. Or maybe he figures anybody with a shirt and tie has got to be a cop or a bill collector.

He gives me the old one-eye and says, "Whattaya want?"

"What would you say if I told you I wanted to rent your establishment for a conve~tion," I snaps back, showing him a little edge and looking into his eyes like I'm trying to read his mind, the same way cops always do. I figure he thinks I could be a cop I might as well use it.

"I'd say you was trying to pull my leg."

"And what would you do about that?"

"I'd tell you I ain't no pansy."

"I ain't heard that word in twenty years."

"So, if that completes your education, tell me your business or let me get back to my magazine."

He slaps the cover of a copy of *True Confessions*, which ain't the unlikeliest thing in the world but which is pretty funny all the same.

"You got a character staying here by the name of Ed Sickle?"

"What for?"

" 'What for' what?"

"What for do you want to know?"

"We don't know each other long enough I want to tell you what business I got with old Ed."

" 'Old Ed,' is it? That means like you been friends for a long time."

"The way you're acting I could ask you the same thing."

"I know old Ed."

"From where?"

"From the last days in the last of the steel mills."

"He moved away."

"That's right. He moved away, then he come back, then he passed through going someplace else, then he lived in PA, then he come back, then he—"

"You know a lot about him."

"I know he was not so lucky."

"How's that?"

"Well, one thing, he couldn't find steady work. No matter where he went he never could find steady work."

"You knew his wife?"

"Sure. Mabel and my wife was good friends before they moved away."

"You knew the kids?"

"Sure."

"How many?"

He looks at me sideways, wondering what that question's all about.

"Three. Two kids of their own and a sister's kid they was taking care of."

"So, you know the Sickles pretty good."

"I just said so."

"So you shouldn't have any trouble remembering if Ed Sickle's staying here."

"Old Ed Sickle, you mean?" he says, making the comment that for a man who pretends to be another man's friend, I don't know too much about Ed Sickle.

"Ed's a common name. So is Sickle. I just wanted to get it straight we was talking about the same fella," I says.

"Sickle's as common as Smith or Jones," he says with a curly lip. "You still ain't told me why I should talk to you."

"I want to ask him some things about his sister-in-law."

"You mean Goldie Hanrahan?"

"How many sisters-in-law does old Ed have?"

"Goldie Hanrahan's dead. It was in the papers and on the news."

"That's what I want to talk to him about," I says, staring holes in his eyes.

I can see his brain cells bumping into each other. He could stonewall me, he could lie to me and protect his old friend, but that could get him into trouble with the law, he thinks.

I start putting two fingers into the handkerchief pocket of my jacket, where a lot of cops keep their badges in a leather flip. "Up to this minute I'm not pushing anything," I says, like in another second, if I got to show him my authority, the nature of our discussion is going to change for the worst so far as he's concerned.

"The fact Goldie Hanrahan's dead'll probably be news to him."

"How's that?"

"He's been drunk ever since he got here. I don't think it even registered when I told him she got killed out there in the woods."

His eyes're flicking all over the place, the way somebody does when they're making up a story. But there was no way I could spot exactly which thing he was saying was the big lie.

"So maybe I can go talk to him, ask him how much he remembers about what and when."

"Room three-B. Just before you get to the stairway on your right at the end of the building."

"Don't bother calling his room," I says.

"Hell, I'm sure old Ed's got no reason not to talk to you."

"You understand what I'm telling you?" I says.

He holds up his hands. "He's on his own."

I give him a nod the way cops do and walked out of the office, down the side of the building to room 3B. I stick my ear against the door. I hear a dull clunk. It could be somebody hanging up the phone. It could be the motel manager don't scare as easy as I thought he would. I knock on the door. A minute later I knock on the door again. Somebody mumbles something like somebody's just been waked up out of a sound sleep. Somebody's a lousy actor. I rattle the knob pretty hard.

"Get the hell outta there," Sickle yells.

I give him some half-yips that sound like words.

I can hear some groans and the complaints of weary bedsprings as he gets off the bed. I can practically see him walking across the room, coughing and spitting into his hand.

He opens up. I can't see him very good because all the drapes're closed and he's standing back from the door.

"Am I talking to Mr. Ed Sickle?" I says.

"Who?" he lisps, since he ain't got any teeth in his mouth.

"Are you Edward Sickle?"

"I'm . . ." He rears back and almost stumbles. Whatever he was going to say he don't say. He coughs again. "Who're you?"

"My name's Jimmy Flannery."

He looks at me like he needs a translation for what I'm saying, weaving slightly on his feet, his hand going up and gingerly touching a big scraped welt on the side of his mouth which has got a little caked blood in the corner. I notice he ain't got the beard Goldie mentioned to Markowitz and Markowitz mentioned to me anymore. I wonder when and why he shaved it off.

"So?" he finally says.

"I'm running an errand for Ray Carrigan."

"Who?"

"Ray Carrigan was a friend of Goldie Hanrahan's."

"You want to come in?" he asks.

"Unless you want to come out."

He sticks his nose up to the door. "Cold as a witch's tit out there. You better come in," he says.

I step inside. The smell of stale beer and whiskey and dirty socks could knock you down.

There's a worn duffel on the floor with some clothes spilling out of it. The wastebasket's full of empty beer bottles and whiskey pints. There's an empty fifth sitting on the nightstand by the bed.

I go over and pull the drapes and open a window. "If you don't mind," I says.

"If you're going to freeze me out of my own room, make it short," he says in this whiny voice.

There's nothing much to him. Life's beat him to his knees so many times it's become his natural way of walking. He goes over to the bed and sits down on the edge of it, staring at his dirty feet like they belong to somebody else.

"You come here to see your sister-in-law?" I asks, sitting down in a straight-backed chair by a little round table near the window.

"No," he says, his voice getting caught in a throatful of phlegm. He coughs it up and looks around for someplace to put it, looking at me sideways like he don't want me to see him doing something that ain't polite. Finally he reaches for the bag the bottle came in and spits into it. "No," he says again. "I was just passing through and I thought as long I was in Chicago I'd look her up."

"After forty years?"

"Sure. Why not?" he snaps a little aggressively, scaring himself and backing off right away. "I mean why shouldn't I want to see my sister-in-law?"

"Just seems funny you'd make the effort," I says. "I mean seeing as how you didn't care that much about her when you gave her kid away."

"Wasn't like that," he says, his face squinching up like he's going to cry. Without his teeth he looks like an infant. Maybe he knows the impression he's giving because he starts rummaging around the junk on the nightstand and finally comes up with his teeth, uppers and lowers. After he pops them into his mouth, he turns to me full face and gives me a big grin like he's trying them out.

I got to admit it does wonders for his kisser, makes him look ten years younger.

"When my Mabel died and my daughter run away, me out of a job and my boy, Earl, nothing but a no-good, what am I supposed to do trying to look for work, keep a leash on Earl—he shouldn't end up in jail—and take care of a nine-year-old kid all at the same time?"

"You could've made the effort. Got in touch with the kid's mother. Let her make the decision did she want the boy back or what."

"Well, I did my best," Sickle says like I'm bad-mouthing him for no reason. "You don't happen to have a little something on you, do you?"

When I don't answer right away he kind of ducks his head and looks coy and says, "You know, a little hair of the dog what bit me."

"I don't get bit by dogs," I says. Then I feel sorry for acting so damned holier-than-thou so I says, "You want to go somewhere and have a drink?"

"Well, I'm awful dry and a little gasoline'd make my engine run better," he says, tapping his forehead. He starts feeling through his pockets. "Only thing is, I don't think I got the price."

"I got the price. Get your shoes on. Maybe you want to wash your face and comb your hair."

"Sure, sure," he says, practically jumping off the bed and running his fingers through hair that's gray and ragged like the stuffing of an old mattress. He's like a kid trying to please his mother so she'll buy him some ice cream.

"It was hard raising three kids after the mills shut down, you can bet," he calls out from the bathroom above the sound of running water.

"Didn't your sister-in-law send money for the boy's support?"

"What did you say?"

He appears in the doorway, his hair dripping wet and shiny black. For a second there he looks another ten years younger.

"I said Goldie paid for her kid's room and board, didn't she?"

"Well, whatever she could've sent didn't go far. Besides, it wasn't often I could get my hands on it or even get Mabel to tell me how much'd come in her sister's letters."

He pops back into the bathroom and comes out a minute later with the sleep washed out of his eyes, his hair combed, and a smile on his face, looking forward to a drink and maybe some good times.

• 22 •

THERE'S AN OLD-TIME SALOON called the Whiskey
Hole half a block down the street.

We walk down to it, Ed taking two steps to my one,
getting ahead of me then backing off like he's afraid he's
going to lose his benefactor.

We push through the doors and it's like getting hit in
the face with a wet bar rag what ain't been rinsed out in
six months. It really is a hole in the wall, dark as a bat's
cave, smelling of a hundred years of beer, pickled eggs,
and pig's feet juice soaked into the soggy wood and worn
linoleum.

The saloon bar's as big as a closet. There's a counter
what takes up one whole wall with a mirror behind it.
The owner's got his stock all pushed up in one spot on
the shelves around the cash register, trying to make it
look like they're loaded with merchandise.

There's two men and one woman strung along the
bar, perched on stools like a bunch of birds tossed and
battered by a storm, feathers all busted and torn, eyes

red from weeping. Nobody, not even the woman, is sitting next to anybody else, but every once in a while one of them will mutter something and look sideways, left or right, to see if anybody's paying any mind.

There's tables and chairs scattered around the center of the floor and two shuffleboards, end to end, across the wall opposite the bar.

It ain't a place where a waiter comes to take your order.

I raise an eyebrow to Sickle and he says, "Rye and a beer chaser?" like, since I'm obviously going to pay for it, he's asking permission.

I step up to the bar while Sickle collapses in a chair like the walk from the motel to the saloon just about done him in.

I come back with the shot glass and the beer in one hand and a ginger ale for me in the other.

Sickle eyes the shot and the beer for a minute like they're rare items from another world. Then he knocks back the shot of rye and shivers as it burns a hole through the sludge in his belly and lights up his brain.

"You sent a postcard to Goldie Hanrahan . . ."

"To my sister-in-law, yes," he says, like he wants to get that relationship straight.

"How come you sent her a postcard after nearly forty years?"

"I just told you why."

"You didn't tell me why. You just asked me why not. Like somebody doesn't correspond with somebody for all that time it's perfectly natural to suddenly up and send them a postcard asking if maybe they'd like to have a meeting."

"I don't see nothing so strange about it. You get old.

You start thinking about the past, you know what I mean? You got nobody to chew the fat about the old times with. About when you was young and things—" He stops short like somebody cut his tongue out of his head. He sits there staring at the empty shot glass. Then he drains the beer.

"She agree to see you?" I asks.

"She called me." He frowns like he's not too sure about that.

"You remember she called you?"

"Sure, why the hell wouldn't I remember she called me if she called me?"

"The manager at the La Salle says you was drunk since the minute you got here."

"Max? What the hell does he know?"

"Well, was you drunk?"

"I could use a topper," he says. "I know it's my turn to buy but I'll have to owe you."

I go get him another boilermaker, but when I bring them back I set them down in front of me and keep a finger on the shot and a finger on the beer chaser.

He starts to reach but I shake my head a little and he understands he's got to play before I pay.

"So Goldie called you," I says.

"Yes."

"What'd she say?"

"She said she didn't have no particular reason to see me again, but she wanted to know what I knew about Charlie."

"You tell her over the phone?"

"You think I'm crazy?" he says, giving me a little curly lip, which makes him wince because his mouth gives him pain when he sneers like that.

"What's that supposed to mean?"

He's in no little confusion. I get the feeling he's not too sure from one minute to the next who he's talking to.

"Hey. Hey, I mean I had a little information she wanted. The least she could do is trade me. Help me out a little bit. You know what I mean?"

He leans forward across the table as though he wants what he's about to say to be confidential, looking sideways at the unsociable drunks perched along the bar like he's afraid they want to listen to what he has to say.

"Hey, you don't suppose there's a connection here, do you?"

"A connection?"

"You know. You don't suppose a person could score a little scag, a little speed, a little something, you know."

So it ain't he's just a lush, which is bad enough, he's got a habit, too.

"You snort it or shoot it or smoke it?" I says.

He gives me a foolish grin. "Hell, I ain't picky."

"Well, I wouldn't know if you could make a score in this place."

"I'll bet you could," he says, grinning slyly like we're in this thing together. "You know how you can tell?"

"No, how can you tell?"

"They got practically no stock on the back bar. Look at the size of this place. You don't keep a place like this running, even in a neighborhood like this, with the money you make off selling shots and drafts. Why don't you shinny up to the bartender, ask him if he's got any fixings?"

I shove the shot glass an inch closer to him.

"Did Goldie come to see you because she wanted to hear about her son? Did you put the arm on her for some dope? Did she tell you no?"

"Christ, I seen her for maybe five minutes."

"Where?"

"Right in my room at the La Salle."

"What did you talk about? Old times?"

"She give me hell for not chasing her down and telling her I was leaving her kid with the Shedds," he says like he's indignant she should've done such a thing.

"Surprised?"

"What the hell you mean? She leaves the kid with her sister. They never even asked me was it okay. She don't come to see the kid for years."

"For a year, year and half."

"She don't even write when I tell her Mabel's dead."

"Maybe she never got the letter."

"That's what she said. I don't believe it. You believe it?"

I push the glass another inch closer to him.

"What else you talk about?"

"Her kid, Charlie. That's funny."

"What's funny."

"She kept on asking about her Baby Boy. Charlie's as old as you and damn near looks as old as me."

"You knew where he was?"

"Hell, yes. Why do you think I wrote her the postcard? Charlie wanted me to set it up for him to meet his mother."

"Is that what you did?"

He nods, his eyes never leaving the shot glass.

"What arrangements did you make?" I asks him.

"It was crazy," he says. "I tried to set it up for here or back at the La Salle or a bar or restaurant of her choosing. I even said how about a park or the Water Tower. She didn't want none of that."

"What did she want?"

"She wanted to meet way the hell out by Saganashkee Slough."

"Why'd she want to do that?"

"I got no idea."

His eyes flick up to mine to get my reaction.

"Hey, I got no idea," he says again, emphasizing each and every word, challenging me to call him a liar.

"What did you do?"

"I said I'd tell Charlie what she wanted him to do, where she wanted him to meet."

"Way out there by Saganashkee Slough?"

"That's right. That's right."

"It's a big place."

"She wrote out directions. Good directions. I gave them to Charlie."

"Where was he?"

"He was waiting for me right here."

"Where's he now?"

"I got no idea. I set up the meeting for him just like I said I would, then I went on about my business." He frowns like thinking's a big effort. "I seem to remember Charlie told me he meant to leave town right after he saw his mother."

"For where?"

"Back to wherever he come from, I suppose."

"You got an address on him?"

"I could maybe remember things a little better if I didn't have this headache. If my mouth wasn't so dry."

I push the glass another inch. He picks it up and bats it back.

"I can't remember no address," he says, and grins like he's scared I'm going to hit him for playing a trick on me.

"So you don't know where Charlie might be right this minute?"

"I ain't got a clue. Why the hell would I want his address? Like they say, no love lost. Hey, you don't mind my asking, what the hell's this all about? Goldie send you over for some reason?"

"Goldie's dead. Ain't you heard?"

He looks at me wide-eyed and openmouthed. He's a lousy actor.

• 23 •

HE'S NOT GOING TO give me anything. I know that. He's going to play drunk on me. Past and present. I got no authority, I got no real clout, so even if he thinks I'm a cop, when I don't take him downtown, when I don't throw him into a holding cell for six, seven hours, when I don't throw a scare into him, he probably thinks he buffaloed a cop. So, that's okay. It ain't really me he thinks he's making a fool out of, it's some cop named Flannery.

I buy him one more and then I walk him back to the La Salle. I get in my car and drive off. But I only drive around a couple of blocks and park on the opposite corner behind a building where nobody from the motel could see me.

I walk up through an alley and stand in the shadows behind a Dumpster. I'm standing there just to satisfy my curiosity. Sure enough, Max, the manager, comes walking up to Sickle's door. He knocks on it a couple of times before Sickle opens up. They have a little discussion which almost becomes an argument.

Sickle finally turns his pockets out, takes a wallet from his back pocket, and opens it up with his thumbs, shaking it upside down in front of Max's nose to show him it's empty.

Max turns away in disgust, throwing a hand back at Sickle like he's telling him to get lost, sore as hell that his good deed, giving Sickle a room, warning him on the phone that I was coming to call, didn't even buy him a dime tip.

I go back to my car and drive around until I find a telephone booth what ain't had the phone ripped out of it. When I find one I call the house.

"It's me," I says.

"My God, for a minute there I thought it was Jack Nicholson calling me for a date," Mary says.

"You hear from Mike?" I asks.

"What's the matter?" she says right away.

"Nothing's the matter."

"You sound so serious."

"I'm going to have that talk with him and I ain't looking forward to it. I called because I thought maybe he called and you invited him over for supper or something."

"You want to talk to him here?"

"No, no. It'd be better if I talked to him alone. Maybe over to his place or Dan Blatna's Sold Out Saloon. I just wanted to check you didn't ask him over for supper. If he was coming over for supper . . ."

"You could postpone talking to him until another day," Mary finishes for me.

"Well, I'm not looking forward to it."

"He's your father."

"That's what I'm saying. It's okay a father asks his son about his girlfriends, but I don't know if it's okay for a son to ask his father about his girlfriends."

"One way or the other it's history we're talking about," Mary points out in this reasonable voice she's got.

"You're right. So Mike didn't call?"

"No, and he's not coming over for supper."

"So I'll go over to his place."

"Why don't you call him first?"

"He could be down on the stoop chewing the fat with this one, that one," I says. "No reason to have him go running up the stairs. I'll just go over and we'll have a talk. So maybe I won't be home for supper on the dot."

"Soup and bacon, lettuce, and tomato sandwiches," she says. "Nothing that can't wait. Take your time."

"Well, then, I'll see you when I see you," I says.

"James?" she says.

"Yeah?"

"Your father loves you as much as you love him. He's not going to get mad at you."

I give her a little laugh. "Or like they say, 'He could shoot me but he can't eat me.' "

I take the long way around over to my father's place in the Fourteenth, where I was born and raised, a little one-room flat he took after he gave up the big house when my mother died—God bless her soul.

I expect to see him out on the stoop chewing the fat with this one or that one like I told Mary, but he ain't there. I look up at the windowsill on the third floor where he puts the telephone if he's out. He's got the ringer cranked up high so he can hear it ring. Then he races upstairs before whoever's calling gives up after maybe eight or nine rings.

I go through the vestibule and up the stairs to the top floor. I'm huffing and puffing by the time I get there. If it was my phone ringing on the windowsill and I was downstairs chewing the fat, I don't think I could make it in nine rings.

I knock on the door and Mike yells, "Ho!"

Half a minute later he opens the door. He's wearing his running suit and his face is ruddy like he just come back from jogging. His hair's dark from the water when he combs his hair. All of a sudden it comes to me that he's my father, so he's an old man to me, but actually he's only about sixty-five, and nowadays that's just a little older than a pup.

"Jimmy, what brings you way the hell over here?"

"What do you mean 'way over'?"

"Well, you know what I mean. I hardly ever see you here at my place anymore. Just passing by?"

"No. I come to see you."

"Come on in. I'll make you a cup of tea."

I go inside the little flat what should be familiar to me but which is all of a sudden not familiar to me.

It's a pretty big room with space for a daybed and a bookcase along one wall. There's an easy chair in a bay window with a floor lamp set just the way he likes it when he reads the paper. Another wall's got a door to a closet and the bathroom. The wall with the entrance also has an alcove with one of them rigs what's a stove, sink, and fridge all in one.

It's very tidy, with shelves he's put up on white metal brackets filled with all the things he needs to make his simple meals or a cup of tea. Which he's doing while I'm looking the place over, wondering if he ever has a woman there.

Like him and Aunt Sada get along very well. The three of them, Charlotte, him, and Sada, get around together a lot, but Mary and me figure if any sparks is going to fly, romantically, they'll fly between Mike and Sada because they're two of a kind, loud and bawdy (Mary says), while her mother, Charlotte's, very quiet and refined.

Or could there be other women from time to time?

It's really very funny how we don't like to think of our mothers and fathers doing that sort of thing—making love, having sex—with even each other, let alone with strangers. It's one of the dumber things about people since if your mothers and fathers hadn't done it at least once per child nobody'd be here to worry about did they do it.

"What are you standing there like a fly looking for a place to land?" Mike says.

"I notice you got no pictures on the walls."

He points the spoon he's got in his hand at a couple of travel posters and one announcing a jazz festival. "What do you call them?"

"You know what I mean. No pictures from the old house."

"They're in storage."

"No pictures of Ma."

Our eyes meet. He's staring at me like he can read my mind.

"It ain't because there's anyone else ever took her place," he says. "I got some in that closet over there."

"What are they doing in the closet?" I asks.

"What's this all about, Jimmy?"

"What's the matter? I just asked you how come you ain't got a picture of Ma on the wall, on a table. Someplace."

"I got a picture someplace," he says.

"Where?"

He pokes hisself on the head and on the chest with his thumb. "Here and here."

The kettle starts to steam. He turns his back on me to make the tea. I go over and sit on the corner of the daybed closest to the windows. It feels like he stirs the sugar in the tea for ten minutes before he brings it over, hands me one, and sits down in his easy chair.

"Okay. Have a swallow and tell me what's eating you."

"I wish Carrigan never asked me to look into Goldie Hanrahan's death."

"Tell him you don't want to do it anymore. Tell him you're sorry but you can't do him the favor. He wants to give you committeeman, then take it away, let him. I don't know if it matters anymore, even if young Daley wins, if you're the committeeman for the Twenty-seventh or if you ain't the committeeman for the Twenty-seventh."

"I know that. I've been saying so for years even though a lot of other people wouldn't say so."

"Meaning me?"

"You for one."

"You're right. Just old men wanting things to stay the same."

"Young men want things to stay the same, too."

"But they don't. Even the past don't stay the same, does it? New facts come to light. You got to rewrite the whole book sometimes, don't you?"

"Well, some of it."

"So what've you found out?"

"Goldie Hanrahan and you . . ." I let it hang there, letting him tell me because that way I wouldn't be questioning my own father like he was some kind of suspect and I was some kind of cop.

"Your mother knew about Goldie Hanrahan," he finally says.

"What did she know?"

"That me and Goldie was what they call an item in the gossip columns. That is if there was anybody around writing about a couple of Irish kids from the Tenth Ward."

"You making jokes, Pa?"

"I'm not making jokes," he snaps back. "What's going on here? Am I supposed to be ashamed for something? I was going out with Goldie Hanrahan when I was picked up for the Korean War. We had an understanding. We wasn't formally engaged or anything like that, but we had an understanding. When I got back we were going to talk serious about getting married. She was only a kid. She couldn't wait. What'd I expect her to do, stay home after work night after night?"

"She had a friend, Sissy Palou."

"Yeah, she had a friend. Sissy was a little wild. You know how she ended up?"

"I met her. She made her living."

"That's what I'd say if you asked me now. Then I said she was nothing but a whore and I didn't want Goldie going around with her."

"So she went around with her anyway?"

"It wouldn't matter if she went out with a girl studying to be a nun. Goldie was pretty. She had this extra something. Men flocked. What could I do? I was a million miles away. I couldn't lock her up. I even told my best buddy to keep an eye on her for me. Take her to a movie if it looked like she was going crazy sitting home alone. Escort her to a dance. Like that."

"Who was this friend?"

"Smith Jarwolski." He sees the surprise on my face. "Hard to believe, right? The way we avoid each other. The way we go at it when we bump into each other."

"If I wanted somebody to keep an eye on a girl of mine, Smith Jarwolski'd be the last man I'd pick," I says.

"Especially he was such a good-looking son of a bitch in that uniform with the leather leggings, up on that goddamn pretty horse."

"What?" I says, like I been bit by a horsefly.

My old man looks startled.

"Jarwolski up on a horse," I says. "I saw that but it didn't register."

"Jarwolski on a horse?"

"No, Jarwolski wearing his uniform with leather leggings."

"Sure. He was in the mounted patrol. Had to be six two or better to be in that outfit. Turned the girls' heads at picnics and parades, I can tell you. The worst choice I could've made for someone to watch out for my interests. He tried to steal her from me. Wanted to marry her hisself."

I stand up.

"Where you going?"

"To have a talk with Smith Jarwolski, superintendent of police," I says. "I got an idea he could've been the father of Goldie Hanrahan's son."

"I had the same idea, but I was wrong."

"How's that?"

"He wanted to marry Goldie but she wouldn't have him. She told me she wouldn't marry Smith Jarwolski if he was the last man on earth."

"That's why I figure he could've been the man who put her in the family way."

• 24 •

IT'S TUESDAY. Goldie's been laid out for people to visit since Sunday. Even with the crowds still coming they figure to bury her Thursday. I got two nights and a day to find her teeth and maybe find out why she got killed.

The next person I want to talk to is Smith Jarwolski. But first I want to see if I got anything but hearsay to go on.

So I use the key to Goldie's apartment again and pick the lock to the little side bedroom like I done before.

Just like I figure, the picture of Smith Jarwolski ain't on the dresser anymore.

I made sure nobody'd see the pictures of my old Chinaman, Chips Delvin, and the Party chairman, Ray Carrigan, and my old man and start asking questions. So Jarwolski did the same for hisself.

There's no trouble getting in to see him. It's like he's been expecting me.

He even stands up when I walk into his office, but I

know it ain't because he wants to be polite, it's because he wants to show me that he's still a big man.

"Have a chair, Flannery," he says, like it's him about to question me.

After I'm sitting down, he sits down.

"So?" he says.

"I never knew you was in the horse patrol," I says.

"You had to be six two or better," he says as though that should explain everything.

"That's what I been told."

He just stares at me. He's ready to talk but he ain't going to give me any help at all.

"Was it the horse what first caught Goldie's eye?" I asks, giving him a little dig.

"Always the wise guy, aren't you, Flannery? Just like your old man. Shanty Irish. Not a pot to piss in but you'll still have lace curtains at the windows. Not a leg to stand on but you'll still make noises like you're the cock of the walk."

"The way I hear it, Mike Flannery had you beat when it came to Goldie Hanrahan. He had to go off to war before you could get your hands on her."

"Let me tell you what kind of arrogant fool your old man was. He asked me to keep an eye on his girlfriend while he goes off to war. What do you think of that? He practically tossed us into each other's arms."

His expression softens up for a second and his eyes get a faraway look. He makes a low noise in the back of his throat like he meant to say something nice but it got stuck there and wouldn't come out. He waves his hand like he's trying to wave away forty years.

"What's the difference?" he says. "It's all dead and buried."

He catches what he's said even before I make the remark but I make it anyway. "Not buried yet. Day after tomorrow it'll be buried."

He turns his face away from me.

"Look, look, look," he says, like he's really dropping his guard and giving in altogether. "We were young. Mike and me and Goldie. I thought I was big and good-looking. He thought he was cute and smart. She was the prettiest girl in the neighborhood. We thought she could've been the prettiest girl in the whole ward."

"You both loved her?"

"We both wanted her. What are we talking about love here? Love comes. I don't know when it comes. I don't think it comes when everybody's running around with hot pants. I don't know if I loved Goldie Hanrahan. Ask your old man did he love her."

"He says he did. He thought he did."

"There you go. He thought he loved her. So why did he give her up so easy when she told him she was going to have another man's kid? Why didn't he tell her he didn't give a damn?"

"She was the one didn't think it was right."

"How come he met your mother and married her six months, maybe a year later? You think your old man married your mother on the bounce and stayed with her all them years because he loved Goldie Hanrahan?"

"He stayed with my mother because they loved each other."

"There you go," he says. "Love comes when it comes. Who knows when? Not always when you think it comes, I can tell you."

I wait for him to tell me what he means by that.

"Maybe it was the horse," he says.

I know that's not what he was going to say. His memories are bouncing all around his head and dropping off his tongue as they come.

"I taught her how to ride. We used to go out to the forest preserve, out by the sloughs."

"Saganashkee Slough?"

"Yes, out there. It was pretty out by the dam."

"Still is. You rape her there?" I says, wanting to sting him some more, wanting him to stop all the soft talk which he could be handing me like honey to a bear.

He jerks his head back like I'd hit him.

"I never had to rape a woman in my life."

"You wouldn't call it rape or even date rape, the way they call it in the magazines and Sunday section of the papers nowadays. Would it sound better the old-fashioned way? Should I ask you if you forced your attentions on her?"

He frowns a little, like he's trying to remember the way it'd been.

"Maybe I did. Maybe I did," he says very soft, like he's talking only to hisself. "Back then every girl was expected to say no even if she didn't mean it."

"And you didn't think Goldie Hanrahan meant it?"

"Not while she was saying no. I found out later on she really meant it."

"How's that?"

"When I found out she was in a family way I asked her to marry me and she wouldn't. She said she didn't want anything to do with me. Said she couldn't stand the sight of me. Said I could be somebody else's Baby Boy."

"What?"

He looks sheepish. "That was her pet name for me. Thinking back, I think she was making fun of me, putting me down. You know what I mean?"

"What happened out at Saganashkee Slough last Wednesday?"

"I got a call from Goldie. It surprised me. She never called me. She hadn't called me except when she was calling for Ray Carrigan in over thirty years. We were always cordial when we met here and there, you understand, but she never called me and I never had any reason to call her."

"She called to tell you Ed Sickle had sent her a postcard and said her kid—your kid—was trying to have a meeting with her?"

"That's right. She wanted to meet him but she didn't want to meet him alone. She wanted me to be there. She said she wanted both of us to be there to see what kind of a man came from the child we'd made."

"You agreed to go?"

"Yes."

"Out to Saganashkee Slough?"

"That's where Goldie wanted the meeting to take place." He gives a little laugh with an edge to it. "That's the sort of thing she'd think up. Wanted to have us all come together at the spot where it'd all started, where we'd . . ."

He stops in the middle and don't pick it up until I give him a little nudge.

"Where you made her pregnant?"

"That's right. And right about the time it happened, too. Early in the morning. Women get crazy ideas, don't they?"

I let it ride because I don't think women do crazy things more than men do crazy things. In fact the crazy things men do usually cause a hell of a lot more damage than the crazy things women do.

"Maybe that's why I decided at the last minute not to make the meeting. Not to be there. Not to play Goldie's little game. What the hell good would it do anybody, after all these years, for us to all get together? What'd she expect, I was going to throw my arms around her and a forty-year-old man and cry about the life we never had together? For Christ's sake, he had nothing to do with me."

It's very quiet in his office. I can hear all kinds of shame and regret skittering around the floor no matter what Jarwolski says.

"About the photograph in Goldie's side bedroom," I says.

He goes into his desk drawer, takes the photo out, and tosses it on the desk in front of me. "You want it?"

"No. I got a couple I took out of there myself."

"I wondered."

"So that's all you can tell me? You don't know if her son ever showed up?"

"No, I don't. You believe me, don't you?"

He's looking at me like my answer to that is important to him.

"You make that anonymous call the other night, telling me to lay off?"

"I should've known better. You're a goddamned junkyard dog, Flannery. You never let go."

I stand up. He don't.

"Why'd you take the photograph?"

"I had easy access to her apartment, running a routine investigation. I figured why not. I figured why not take it out of circulation so it didn't fall into the wrong hands. So it didn't get back to my wife and kids."

"Would it've embarrassed you if they knew you'd knocked up a dumb, young Irish girl forty years ago?"

I know Jarwolski married into society and I want to hurt him one more time. He winces a little. Maybe he does it on purpose to give me the satisfaction, like he wants to pay off and keep the books between us even.

I walk across the floor.

"Did you get a little pain in your heart when you found out your father loved another woman before he loved your mother?" he says, giving it back.

I don't say anything, I just keep on walking until I'm at the door.

"Well, I didn't see any reason to give my wife a little pain in her heart, forty years ago or no forty years ago," he goes on.

There's something in his voice that makes me feel sorry for him. Here he is an old man trying to save his wife a little distress for what a young man did long ago. Also I get the feeling he wonders what would've happened if Goldie'd said, yes, she'd marry him, and they'd raised that kid, and maybe a couple more, together.

"By the way," I says, turning with my hand on the knob, "you know about the initials in Goldie's fillings?"

"What're you talking about?"

"Goldie was a sentimental woman with a tender heart and a little treasure of old memories. She had the initials of three people put in her teeth. Ray Carrigan's, I think."

"He was very good to her over the years," Jarwolski says.

"Mike Flannery."

"So she never stopped loving your old man."

"And Baby Boy. So, who knows. She could've loved you, too, even if she wouldn't marry you. Women do crazy things sometimes."

• 25 •

WHAT I GOT is a lot of aging men with the past all tangled up in the present. Any one of them, even my old man, could have a reason for not wanting the old scandal involving a sixteen-year-old beauty and an illegitimate baby surfacing forty years later. But I can't get myself to believe any one of them would have a reason to kill her over it.

It starts to snow.

I drive over to Delvin's house, knock on the door, and when Mrs. Thimble opens up, I go through the same ritual of verbal abuse for not wearing my galoshes that Mrs. Banjo used to put me through.

Finally I'm sitting in the parlor in the big easy chair looking at Delvin sleeping in his chair. He's like a big tree what just fell over. I expect to see birds fly out of his wispy hair.

I clear my throat and he starts awake.

Before he can ask me if I want a refreshment and before he can yell for any, Mrs. Thimble's there with two hot drinks on a tray. I'd like to know how he got her turned around so she's so quick and polite.

After she leaves the room I do a number with my eyes and a jerk of the head which Delvin understands right away.

He grins in perfect satisfaction. "Handling women is an art, Jimmy. One day, when you're old enough, I may impart the secret."

"Did you always have the gift or did someone give it to you?"

"I was born knowing. At least that's what all the ladies I've ever known've told me."

"Even Goldie Hanrahan?"

"Goldie was a girl. A child. A waif."

"You never had anything romantic with her?"

"It depends largely on what you mean by romance. If you mean sex, there was never any of that between us."

"Your choice or hers?"

"It was precluded by the demands and delights of friendship."

"Did you give her a helping hand?"

"I pulled some strings. I was sorry after."

"Why's that?"

"I gave the girl a taste of prestige and power. I'm not sure that such apparent treasures don't corrupt women more than men." He reads my face or my mind because then he says, "I know all about the equality of sex and gender, Jimmy. Nor am I in complete disagreement with their demand for it nowadays. But this was then. Goldie was a child of the mills. She'd not have been as rich or powerful as a wife and mother, but I believe in my heart that she'd've been a darn sight happier."

I hand him the picture of him and Goldie I took from the dresser. He looks at it for a long minute and his eyes fog over a little bit.

"She treated me like the father she never had and I gave her bad advice."

"What was that?"

"I told her not to marry Smith Jarwolski." He waves his hand impatiently like I've already asked how come and he's angry with hisself because he's got no answers. "Five years later I told her to let her sister raise her kid."

I keep my mouth shut.

"Even old Chinamen make mistakes," he says, then drinks half of his hot whiskey and water. "It's been mild so far, James, but it's going to be a long, cold winter."

I stand up to go and hand him my toddy. "Take care of yourself, Mr. Delvin, and be sure to keep warm."

Marilyn O'Connell's there behind her desk doing her nails. She smiles at me when I walk in the door like we're a couple of school kids and I'm on my way in to get hell from the principal. Come to think of it, I suppose it starts way back in grammar school, the way some people like to see other people get it.

Mistinguette's laying on her rug. She don't look pregnant to me but I already know that a week's too soon to tell.

"You have an appointment?" Marilyn asks me.

"Do I need an appointment?"

"I don't suppose." She hits the intercom switch and when Carrigan growls, "What is it?" she tells him I'm waiting to see him and he tells her to send me in. He don't even tell her to ask me do I want a coffee.

He's sitting behind his desk looking mean.

"I know all about what your dog did to my dog," he says.

"I been told," I says.

"How come you didn't tell me?"

"I thought you wanted me paying attention to something more important than did my dog do it to your dog."

"She's a champion," he says. "What kind of dog is your dog?"

"A poodle," I says.

"Oh?" he says. "A good one?"

"A rare one."

"How's that?"

"Unusual markings."

"Mixed breed?"

"No. I understand the kennel club's going to designate the colors and pattern as a special class. You know like they done with all the different kind of spaniels they got nowadays."

"Who told you that?"

"Well, I don't remember exactly who told me that. It could've been Mary. It's Mary's dog, you know. I mean he just hangs out with me, but he's Mary's dog and she's very keen on breeding and all like that."

"So maybe if what your dog did to my dog makes puppies, it wouldn't be an altogether terrible thing?"

"They'll be different, you can bet your life on that. About Goldie Hanrahan," I says, getting his mind off dogs and poodles what look like Alfie which he ain't even seen yet.

"Before we get off the subject," he says, "when can I see your dog?"

"Whenever you want."

"How about you bring him to the cemetery and I can have a look at him after we bury Goldie?"

"God keep her," I says, which means I don't really answer him about giving him a look at Alfie so soon.

"You find out anything about what happened to Goldie?" he asks.

I take the photo of him and Goldie when they was

young out of my pocket and put it on his desk just like I done with Delvin.

"Where'd you get that?"

"In a little locked bedroom Goldie had in her flat."

"I knew about that bedroom but I never been in it," he says. He reads my expression and adds, "She let me know it was private when she gave me the key to her place. I respected that."

"But you didn't tell me to respect her privacy when you asked me to nose around."

He don't say nothing for half a minute. Then he says, "I must've forgot."

"I don't think you forgot, Mr. Carrigan. I think you wanted to know if there was anything in that room could put the finger on you for what happened forty years ago."

"If I was worried, I would've walked in myself."

"Oh, no. First of all, I don't think you'd know how to pick a lock, and if you did manage to break in, somebody'd find out about it. Second, you gave Goldie your word."

"If I gave her my word why would I break it giving you the key?"

"Because that's the way a politician's head works. Like a lawyer's. Sideways. From an angle. It ain't what you do, it's the way that you do it. It ain't what you say, it's the way that you say it. I bring you something like what I just brung you and you say, 'Surprise, surprise, whoever would've thought it.' "

His eyes narrow and these bright spots of color pop out on his cheeks. Carrigan, even at his age, ain't a man to cross and I just crossed him. I just all but called him a liar. I showed him the gravy on his tie that proved he was a slob.

"When I saw you out at Saganashkee Slough it was the second time you was there that morning," I says.

He gives it up like the air going out of a balloon. Mike and Jarwolski gave it up the same way, glad to have the truth come out after all these years. Glad to admit what fools they'd been. I guess we're all running around looking for somebody to give us absolution. I been it enough times to know.

"I was there," he says.

"How come?"

"Goldie called me the night before to tell me all about her son coming back to see her. She told me how Smith Jarwolski promised to be there and then how he called to break the promise. She didn't want to meet her son all by herself."

"Why was that?"

"She gave me the feeling that she didn't completely believe it was really him."

"She thought somebody was running a game on her?"

"It was a possibility. After all, she hadn't seen the boy since he was seven or eight."

"Didn't she trust her mother's intuition?"

"Would you believe in mother's intuition after more than thirty years?"

"I wouldn't but . . ."

"I doubt many mothers would either, no matter what they say. So I said I'd be there when she met the man."

"Didn't you think Saganashkee Slough was a funny place to meet?"

"I did and I said it was a damn foolish thing for her to've set up after she told me why she'd done it that way."

"Wanting to stick the knife into Jarwolski one more time?"

"Ah, for Christ's sake, she loved the man. She probably wanted to meet there because she wanted to make it symbolic or something."

"So you went and met the son?"

"I went. I drove the hell out there myself in the dark. I don't know that part of the county. I never went hiking, horseback riding, anything like that. I went out there and parked on a Hundred and seventh where Goldie told me to."

"I know the spot."

"Yeah, I know you do. So you know you got to walk through the weeds and brush and trees down to the dam."

"I was there."

"I know you were," he snaps, like he's annoyed at me for butting in. "I got lost," he goes on, like he's ashamed to say so. "I got lost in them dark goddamned woods. I heard angry voices. I heard a horse yell or whinny or whatever the hell they do. I heard Goldie scream. I started to run. Goldie screamed again. Then I heard a smash and somebody hitting the ground and hoofbeats going away. Somebody went crashing through the underbrush."

"I guess he heard you crashing through the underbrush, too."

"I guess so," Carrigan says, like he's slowing down and out of breath after a long run through the woods.

"So you never got to see who it was?"

"It took me three, maybe four minutes to find my way to where she was."

"You think it was her son?"

He hesitates. Then he says, "I thought it could've been Smith Jarwolski."

"You thought Jarwolski was the one killed Goldie Hanrahan?"

"Even if he isn't, the son of a bitch has something coming to him for what he did to her forty years ago."

If words were acid there'd be holes burning in his desk top.

He's hated Jarwolski all this time so bad that he even tried to convince himself that Jarwolski'd do injury to Goldie, and even failing proof of that, Carrigan just wanted his enemy dropped in the boiling oil one way or another.

He sees me staring at him and turns his head away. The light and shadows falls on his face a certain way and all of a sudden he's a young man. It comes to me that all these young men was in love, one way or another, with this slip of a girl.

And it comes to me that if a trick of light could make an old man look young, there's plenty more tricks could make a young man look old.

· 26 ·

I RUN DOWNSTAIRS and jump in my car. I'm doing thirty before I leave the curb. I hit the pedal all the way over to the La Salle Motor Lodge.

Having missed out on the follow-up with the kids what Koslow let get away before anybody thought to look in their pockets for Goldie Hanrahan's teeth, I'm afraid I'm the one who lets Ed Sickle—or whoever the hell he is—get away.

I'm looking right, left, front, and back. I'm making the lights. I'm shaving them by an eyelash. All I need is a cop stopping me. I get to the La Salle and leave an inch of brake lining in front of Sickle's room.

I scramble out and rap on his door. There's no answer. I stick my ear against it but I can't hear a squeak or a flush. I rap again and give it another thirty seconds before I try the handle. It don't budge. I put my shoulder to it.

"Hey!" somebody shouts.

Max, the manager's, walking over to me. He's in a hurry.

"What the hell you think you're doing?" he asks me.

"I'm trying to wake up your friend, Ed Sickle."

"That's funny. I'd swear you was trying to break down my door."

"I ain't getting no answer. I'm worried he could be dead."

"What makes you say that?"

"I got reason to believe his friend Charlie Shedd might've done him an injury."

"Who?"

"The guy what come to visit Ed in his room."

"Nobody come to visit Ed."

"How can you be sure about that?"

"I got no night man. I work the office all by myself twenty-four hours a day."

"How about when you sleep?"

"I'm a light sleeper. I hear every damn car pulls in."

"He could've come on foot."

He shrugs, giving me that possibility. "I couldn't say. But you're wasting your time trying to bust down my door anyway. Ed's long gone."

"How long?"

"This morning. He trotted the hell out of here this morning."

"What was he driving?"

Max gives me a grin. "He come on foot."

"I want to tell you something," I says. "When I come here the first time I tell you not to call Sickle's room because I mean to surprise him, but you go ahead and warn him I'm coming anyway."

"I don't know about that," he says.

"Well, I know about it."

"Is that what you wanted to tell me?"

"No. What I wanted to tell you was if you're lying to me about Sickle leaving, it'll mean you screwed me twice. You know the old saying. 'Screw me once, shame on you. Screw me twice, shame on me.' "

He takes out his master key, shoves past me, and unlocks the door, swinging it wide with this big gesture like he's opening up his heart and soul. It's empty all right. Sickle and his bag're long gone.

I walk back to my car, figuring I blew it. I'm standing there wondering what I can do next, staring down the street toward the Whiskey Hole. The sign's blinking from a bad connection and it catches my attention. Just like I know the sun's going to set and rise again I know that it caught Sickle's attention, too, and I doubt he could resist it.

I trot on down to the saloon and get hit in the face with the bar rag again when I walk through the door.

It looks like the same three barflys is perched on the stools. It looks like they never moved.

Sickle's over at the same table we had before.

I slide into the chair across from him. It takes him a while to realize somebody's sitting with him. It takes him another while to focus me in.

"Hi there, buddy," he says, giving me a grin and a wave of the hand. "Hey, I owe you a couple, don't I? From the other day? I hate a man what leeches off another man in a saloon. I mean a son of a bitch'll do that'll suck his own toes. What can I get you?" He starts to struggle to his feet. I put out a finger and tap him in the chest hard enough to make him fall back. It don't take much. "Hey," he says, "they got no table service in this joint, what do you think? You got to belly up to the bar and carry your own."

"I'm okay. I don't want nothing," I says.

"I won't sit with a man what won't have a drink with me," he says.

"All right, I'll get it," I says.

He shoves a bill at me from a small bunch of money in front of him. "Take it out of this," he says, looking at me like he expects I'm going to insult him by buying my own.

I pick up the buck and go get myself a ginger ale.

When I come back he's counting his fingers. "I got enough for five more shots," he says.

"Where'd you get the money?" I asks.

"What?"

"You were broke just yesterday. You had to pay for your room at the La Salle."

"Credit card."

"You been buying drinks for yourself today."

"Credit card."

"In this joint? Don't make me laugh. Where'd you get the money?"

"I borrowed some from Max."

"I don't think so. Max was trying to get some money out of you yesterday for doing you the favor."

"What favor?"

"Warning you that I was on my way. He didn't like it when you showed him empty pockets."

"You know a lot, you do. You think I'd tell a son of a bitch like Max everything about my business? You think I'd tell him how much money I had on me?"

"Where'd you get the money?"

"Hey, what the hell's your name, Johnny One Note?"

"All I got to do is walk around the neighborhood, up one street, down another. Go into all the pawn shops—how many can there be around here?—and find the one where you pawned Goldie Hanrahan's bridgework."

I never see a man look so scared or sober up so fast. He starts breathing fast and hard.

"If you say you got to make a run for the bathroom to get sick, let me tell you that I'll be right behind you. I'll even hold your head."

He swallows two or three times. "Oh, Christ," he moans.

"So, now we got that out of the way, the next thing I want you to tell me is who the hell you are."

"What the hell you mean? I'm Ed Sickle." He tries to make it bold but it comes out weak.

"No, you ain't. You ain't old enough to be Ed Sickle. You know who I think you are?"

He just stares at me like he figures I know everything already anyway, so he'll just sit and listen.

"I think you're . . ." I hesitate, watching his mouth so I can read every twitch. "Ch . . . ," I start to say, then swallow it quick when I see this little smile start, like he figures I don't know everything after all, and say, "Earl Sickle," instead. "You're Charlie's cousin."

The expression on his face tells me everything.

"You figured you could be Ed Sickle when you met Goldie Hanrahan in a motel with the drapes closed, your teeth out, and a beard on your face. Later on, with your teeth in, without your beard, and maybe with a hairpiece you could play you were Charlie Shedd, her Baby Boy. After all, thirty years has passed by and a lot of water's gone under the bridge. Besides, she'd want to believe what she wanted to believe. Is that what you figured? Was that the game?"

He grins this twisted little grin. "You think you're so goddamned smart. I had it worked out better'n that. I had a friend was going to play the part of Charlie Shedd— Charlie Hanrahan—Charlie whoever."

"A friend?"

"The son of a bitch got cold feet and run out on me."

"And you went through with it yourself?"

He shrugs like what the hell did I think he was supposed to do. Just give it up? Just give it up after all the trouble he'd gone through?

"I figured I could pull it off. I figured I could make it short and sweet. I figured she'd be glad to give her long-lost son a couple of bucks. I ain't had a good time of it."

I hate to preach or make remarks about the way another person lives but I couldn't help it. I tap the shot glass and says, "And you never will until you give it up."

"Fuck you," he says, like what do I know about it.

"Did she take one look at you and know right away you weren't her Baby Boy? Did she tell you the best thing you could do was go back to wherever you come from?"

"I had to take a taxi way the hell out there. It wasn't cheap," he says, very indignant, like anything that happened to Goldie Hanrahan after that happened because he had to take a taxi out to Saganashkee Slough and then she told him he was a fake and he'd have to walk all the way the hell back to Chicago.

"You had money for a cab but you didn't have the price of a drink, so I had to buy?"

He gives me the grin of the experienced sponger. "No buses that hour." Then he gets serious again.

"I didn't mean to hurt her. I just wanted to scare her a little bit for being so goddamn mean to me. I just wanted to grab her wrist and make her listen to me, be fair to me. I mean she left her goddamn brat with my old man and my ma and that meant less for me. There was nothing to start with but that meant there was just that much less for me."

"She hit you with her riding crop?" I asks.

He touches his wounded mouth and cheek.

"That was a lousy thing for her to do."

"That why you started to rape her?"

"What?"

"Her pants was unbuttoned and her belt undone."

"I was trying to give her some air. I thought she was only hurt. I never ... Jesus Christ ... I never would ..." He runs down and wipes his mouth with the back of his hand.

"I got to ask you one more thing," I says. "How come Goldie agreed to meet Charlie way out there at Saganashkee Slough? How'd you manage to get her way out there?"

"I never," he says. "I never even heard of the goddamn place. That's where she wanted the meeting to take place. See that?"

"See what?"

"I wanted to meet right here in this bar. Right back here where the light ain't so good. If she didn't pick the place she picked what happened to her probably never would've happened."

I turn to the bar and get the bartender's eye.

"Come over here a minute, will you?" I says.

"We got no waitress," he says.

"Come over here anyway and I'll tip you like you was one. Just get the hell over here."

He takes his own sweet time about it.

"I didn't want to yell it," I says. "I want you to call the police while I sit here with my friend. I don't want you to call just anybody. I want you to call Smith Jarwolski hisself and tell him I got the man what killed Goldie Hanrahan."

• 27 •

JARWOLSKI HISSELF comes with a couple of uniforms and picks up Earl Sickle.

I ask them to search him and see if he's got a pawn ticket on him. He has. It's tucked in his wallet.

"You want a receipt for this, Earl, or is it okay I take it?" I asks.

"Do what you want," he says.

After they take him away, Jarwolski and me sit down.

"Is that pawn ticket evidence?" he asks.

"It could be. He pawned Goldie's bridgework."

"Give me the ticket," Jarwolski says.

"Carrigan says he'd like her buried with her teeth."

"What do I care what Carrigan wants?"

"It'd be a nice thing to do."

"You think he killed her on purpose?" Jarwolski asks.

I shrug my shoulders. "What do I know? What does anybody know?

"Maybe Goldie Hanrahan loved you but maybe she

figured you was going to marry her just because you got her pregnant and that wasn't good enough for her. Maybe she was sorry for it later on or maybe she got bitter about it when she got older and wanted to rub your nose in it when she thought her son, Charlie'd, come back to see her. Maybe she wanted you to hurt like she'd been hurting, or maybe she hoped, when she saw the three of you was together, that it would somehow make things better if not all right. Maybe she just wanted to see if there was a resemblance."

"I'm not asking you what you think about Goldie or me. I'm asking you if you think this Earl Sickle killed her."

"Something killed her. Events killed her. Unforeseen consequences killed her. What I'm saying is that it all started back when you was all young."

"Do you think he killed her, goddammit?" he shouts at me.

"I don't think you're going to have enough for the grand jury to bring down a true bill. I don't think you'll even have enough to get the district attorney interested. I think it was an accident just like Sickle says it was."

"You're probably right," Jarwolski says after a little while.

"You going to do something about it?"

"Like what?"

"Like seeing that Earl Sickle has a fatal accident on his way out of town?"

"I don't do things that way, Flannery."

"I was hoping you didn't do things that way, Jarwolski."

He stands up. "You're a piece of work, you are, Flannery."

"It's okay I get Goldie's teeth back for her?"

"You Irish are a bunch of sentimental pains in the ass," he says. "You'll have to sign an affidavit swearing to the source of the ticket."

"I'll be happy to do that."

He walks out, leaving me with the ticket.

It's got the pawn shop's name on it. It's just around the corner.

I go get Goldie's bridgework and take it over to the funeral parlor. She don't look much different after the cosmetician puts it in her mouth. I didn't really expect her to.

But when Carrigan arrives for the service and sits down near the head of the coffin, the fact she's going to be buried with her teeth seems to please him.

The service is short and sweet, the usual lawyer's brief about what a nice person is going to her rest, like he's making the case for her in front of the judge's bench up in heaven.

After that we get into the procession and follow Goldie out to the cemetery. I'm in my car right behind Carrigan and park behind him at the bottom of the hill where the grave's waiting up the slope.

We stand around the grave while Goldie gets another send-off.

After it's over, Carrigan and Marilyn and me walk down the grassy slope together.

"One more thing, Flannery," Carrigan says, "you promised me a look at that fancy poodle of yours."

Marilyn gives me a look but I put on my angel face.

"My pleasure, Mr. Carrigan," I says, and when we reach my car I open the door and tell Alfie to jump out.

He don't want to at first. I can tell he's embarrassed

because I had a dog barber give him one of them fancy trims, the topknot, pom-poms, and anklets, just like all the show poodles got.

"Oh, my God," Marilyn says.

"Ain't he a beauty?" I says.

"Well, he's certainly different," Carrigan says, making up his mind to be pleased about it.

"Thank you, Mr. Carrigan," I says.

"Call me Ray, Jimmy," Carrigan says. "Call me Ray."